"You'll let me know if you hear anything about Jared?"

"Of course," Connor said. "But before I go, I want to take a look around. Make sure it's safe."

The fact that the gunmen had seemed like paid hit men weighed on his mind. Professionals typically had backup plans as well as clear motivation to keep trying. They would come after Jared again. Or Naomi. Or both.

He walked through to the kitchen. A breakfast nook with a bay window afforded a view of the lake. "Beautiful view."

Naomi followed him, dropping her phone and purse on the countertop. "I start and end my days right here so I can enjoy the view as much as possible."

"I'm going to check the rest of the first floor and then I'll look upstairs," Connor said.

He was halfway to the second floor when he heard the loud bang of an explosion from the kitchen.

"Naomi!" He sprinted down the stairs, charging toward the quickly expanding inferno.

"Naomi!" he called out again.

She didn't answer.

Jenna Night comes from a family of Southern-born natural storytellers. Her parents were avid readers and the house was always filled with books. No wonder she grew up wanting to tell her own stories. She's lived on both coasts but currently resides in the Inland Northwest, where she's astonished by the occasional glimpse of a moose, a herd of elk or a soaring eagle.

Visit the Author Profile page at LoveInspired.com.

FUGITIVE IN HIDING

JENNA NIGHT

LOVE INSPIRED SUSPENSE
INSPIRATIONAL ROMANCE

LOVE INSPIRED SUSPENSE
INSPIRATIONAL ROMANCE

Recycling programs
for this product may
not exist in your area.

ISBN-13: 978-1-335-58854-8

Fugitive in Hiding

Copyright © 2023 by Virginia Niten

For questions and comments about the quality of this book, please contact us at CustomerService@Harlequin.com.

Love Inspired
22 Adelaide St. West, 41st Floor
Toronto, Ontario M5H 4E3, Canada
www.LoveInspired.com

Printed in U.S.A.

I have set the Lord always before me: because he is at my right hand, I shall not be moved.
—*Psalm* 16:8

To my mom, Esther.

ONE

"Sis, I'm in trouble. I need your help."

Naomi Pearson's heart sped up as she pressed the phone closer to her ear to better hear her brother's voice. "What's wrong?"

She continued threading her way through the crowded cobblestone walkway on Indigo Street in the historic section of downtown Range River, Idaho. Thursday nights were the unofficial start of the weekend and the partyers were already out in force. That's why she'd come down here looking for Jared. She was afraid he'd fallen back into old habits and was hanging out at Club Sapphire.

"I'm not sure what's going on," he said, fumbling over the words.

Oh man. He must be drinking again. That would explain why he'd skipped his court date earlier today—which was the reason she'd started searching for him.

"Are you in the nightclub?" she asked, stopping as she reached Club Sapphire's gem-colored door.

"No." His single-syllable response was drawn out, ending in something like a wail. "They drugged me. Something in my drink."

"Who?" Naomi demanded. "Who drugged you?" She and Jared might be well into adulthood, but she would always be the big sister. She still felt guilty over those years in his early teens when she hadn't been around and he'd gotten off on the wrong foot when it came to figuring out how to live life. But she would be here for him now.

"I don't know who they are," he said, choking up. "I don't know what is happening, but this is bad. They've got guns."

Guns. Naomi's blood chilled. "*Where* are you?"

"A house. On the river. Near the old sawmill. I don't know the actual address."

He was west of where Naomi was right now, just two or three blocks away. She started jogging in his general direction. "What color is the house?"

"Blue with white trim."

Naomi put her phone on speaker and broke into a full-out run. She didn't know what her brother had gotten mixed up in, but she would not let him down again.

"Can you get outside?" she asked. She wanted to call 9-1-1, but she was afraid to hang up on Jared. He could lose consciousness, or the mysterious threatening people could do something very bad to him. There wasn't much she could do for him from the other end of a phone line, but at least he'd know he wasn't alone.

"I'm already outside. On the back lawn, facing the river."

"If you're already outside, get up and run away!" she shouted into the phone. Was he so addled that he hadn't thought of that?

"My legs." He sounded breathless. "I'm trying to get up and move but I'm unsteady."

Naomi was closing in on the house now. She could see it in the early evening light.

"I think I've found where you are," she said into the phone. She slowed down as she left the sidewalk and headed toward the side yard. Winded, she fought to recover her breath as she crouched down and moved toward the back of the house, hoping she would be out of sight of anyone who might be watching. She wanted to make sure this was the right location before she called the police. She muted her phone to make certain she wouldn't be noticed if something bad was happening.

Just before she moved to look around the corner of the house, she heard yelling and the sounds of a struggle, followed by a metallic snap, like a gun with a suppressor being fired. Nearly sick to her stomach with fear, she cautiously peered around the corner.

Her brother yelled "No!" as two men grappled with him. Jared twisted and turned and fought to break free from the grasp of the men who were holding on to him.

In an instant, Naomi's mind registered two horrifying sights. Her brother had a gun in his hand. And there was a man lying on the patio, blood pooling around his head.

Jared! No! Quickly, she shifted those thoughts to a prayer. *Lord, please. Stop my brother and don't let that poor man be dead.*

She fumbled with her phone, intending to end her call with Jared and dial 9-1-1, when she heard her brother issue a feral growl. She looked up to see him put forth a sudden burst of energy and shove himself backward and away from the man lying prone on the patio and the two men who were holding his arms, but his efforts didn't work.

In the next moment she realized something

was off. She wasn't seeing what she'd initially *thought* she was seeing.

The black-haired man to Jared's right yanked her brother's hand forward and squeezed the gun's trigger, firing one more shot into the poor soul lying on the ground.

Jared screamed as if his heart were breaking and it became clear to Naomi that her brother hadn't willingly killed the man. Instead, these two thugs had put a gun in his hand and physically forced him to pull the trigger. More than once.

Jared Santelli, nonviolent man with an admittedly checkered past, a person desperately trying to overcome his personal failings, had been drugged to make him more easily controlled, and then he'd been framed for murder.

Unfortunately, in the terror and anxiety of the moment, Naomi squeezed her phone and accidentally unmuted it. It was still on speaker and she hadn't disconnected her call with Jared. Loud sounds poured out and she quickly muted it again, but it had been just enough noise for one of the assailants to notice it. The shorter attacker, with long brown hair, turned his head and looked directly at her.

For a moment she felt completely numb with fear.

"I called the police," she finally managed to shout. "I saw what you did. Jared didn't want to shoot that gun. You forced him to. *You* shot that man."

Probably not the smartest thing to do, calling out the thug, but she had no weapon and no option other than to bluff. She could only hope a neighbor had heard gunshots. Maybe someone had called the cops and officers would be arriving at any second.

The assailants exchanged glances and then let go of Jared. "Took you long enough to get here," the black-haired one said before taking a shot at her.

Naomi ducked.

Afraid for her brother, she risked another peek in their direction only to see the gunmen running around the other end of the house and out of sight.

Relief mixed with astonishment at the realization her threat had worked.

Though he was unsteady and weaving a little, Jared had managed to stay on his feet. As soon as the assailants were out of sight, he leaned over to carefully drop the gun that was still in his hand onto the ground. Then he quickly stepped away as if it were a serpent that could bite him.

"Hey, are you all right?" Naomi called out as she cautiously made her way toward him while scanning the area to make sure the bad guys were truly gone.

Her brother stumbled toward her and grabbed her so tightly she could hardly breathe. "It's Kevin Ashton," he said, gesturing toward the figure on the ground. It took her a minute to place the name. He was Jared's sponsor. A man who helped him stay sober.

What in the world had happened here? She shook off the question. She could get answers later. Right now she needed to hurry over to Mr. Ashton to see if there was anything they could do for him. As she drew closer it became fairly obvious that the man was dead, but Naomi felt for a pulse and respiration just to make sure. Her fears were confirmed.

"I'm sorry," she said, looking up at Jared, his eyes wide as saucers and his arms crossed tightly over his chest.

Her brother nodded and then wiped his eyes with the sleeve of his jacket. "He was a good man. He didn't deserve this."

Nobody deserved this.

"Okay, now I'm *really* going to call the cops," she announced.

"Wait," Jared said, grabbing her arm urgently. "Call Connor Ryan first. Please."

"Connor?" The word came out a little strangled.

"Yes. Anybody at Range River Bail Bonds could help, but I would really like Connor to come here. You saw what happened. You know my record. The police aren't going to believe the truth. Not at first. I have gunshot residue on my hands and my prints are all over the gun. If they arrest me, Connor can get me out of jail. Or at least he can try. *Please.* Call him first."

Connor Ryan. Naomi had been back in her hometown for nearly two months and she'd managed to avoid him. She'd hoped to go the rest of her life avoiding him, but apparently that was too much to ask.

Bam!

At the sound of gunfire Jared leaped onto Naomi, knocking her to the ground and out of the line of fire.

Bam!

The second shot hit the side of the house, ricocheted off and blasted a scar across a brick in the patio.

Naomi and Jared were already rolling and crawling and making every desperate move they could to get out of view and into the cover

of the bushes and shrubs. When they came
to a halt, Naomi carefully lifted her head to
look in the direction the shots had come from.
She could see the dark-haired assailant beside
the house in a shooter's stance, scanning the
grounds to see where she and Jared had gone.
Beyond him, out near the street where he could
keep watch, was the second gunman.

Naomi mentally kicked herself.

She was an idiot. Of course they hadn't been
scared off by her threat. They'd just pretended
that they were to draw her out and make it easier to shoot her and her brother. It would be a
simple thing for the thugs to melt away into
the darkness the second they saw or heard a
cop car approaching.

The dark-haired man suddenly settled his
gaze directly in Naomi's direction. She winced
as she realized that her movement might have
caused moonlight to glint off her glasses,
drawing the gunman's attention.

"Can you run?" she whispered to Jared.

"I think so. Feels like whatever they slipped
into my coffee is starting to wear off."

Starting to. So not completely. *Please, Lord,
protect us.*

The gunman began moving toward them.
Naomi gave her brother a slight shove. "Go!"

"Which way?"

She gestured in the direction of the shuttered sawmill surrounded by forest at the end of the street. "That way. Now *move*!"

Naomi took off running, mindful of Jared by her side, alert to any signs of him stumbling due to the drugs that he'd been slipped. She pushed through the hedge into the backyard connected to the house next door and then kept going, sticking to the shadows and clumps of trees and bushes on the property as much as possible all while making sure that her brother remained hot on her heels.

She didn't dare slow down and knock on a door to ask for help. She could hear the thugs close behind them. The one who'd been acting as a lookout must have joined the dark-haired gunman. The criminals were breaking branches and breathing heavily as they tried to catch up with Naomi and Jared.

After clearing the final residential yard, Naomi crossed a narrow dirt road and came face-to-face with a twelve-foot-high chain-link fence. On the other side, beyond the tall pines near the fence, was the old Lexford Sawmill. It had been permanently closed back before Naomi had even been born. She and her friends used to sneak onto the property to play when they were kids.

"What are you going to do now?" the long-haired thug called out as she hesitated in front of the fence. She could hear mockery in the criminal's tone. At the same time she could hear his and his partner's footfalls slow down. The creeps thought they had them cornered.

She sprang at the fence and started climbing. Fast. After all, the fence had been there when they were kids, too. It was hardly her first time climbing it. Jared managed it easily, as well.

Bam! Bam! Bam!

The gunmen started firing, bullets striking the links of the fence, sending off sparks and shards of metal around Naomi's hands and face. She felt a sudden strike and a burning sensation on her right shoulder, but the pain wasn't unbearable and she kept going.

She made it over the top and dropped down. Jared hit the ground seconds later and they sprinted into the forested area in front of them.

Gunfire continued as Naomi led the way to the old admin building, where they could hide.

"Why were they shooting at *you*?" Jared said as they stepped inside the building and dropped to the floor, taking a desperately needed few moments to catch their breath. "What's going on?"

"What are you talking about?" Naomi said. "They were after both of us."

"But just now, when we were on the fence, nearly all the shots were aimed at you. They fired at me, but it seemed like you were the main target."

She turned toward him, thinking through what he'd said and trying to make sense of his words.

Took you long enough to get here, the black-haired criminal had said to her earlier. She hadn't had time to process those words until now.

She turned to her brother. "Have you ever seen those two men before?"

Jared shook his head. "Not before today. I was meeting Kevin in a coffee shop when those two creeps wandered over and joined our conversation. They acted like they needed counseling and of course Kevin was willing to help them."

"But who would come after us? Who would want us dead? And *why*?"

"I don't know." Jared shook his head. Then he stopped and stared at her. "But what if whoever is behind this has connections in the county jail? I could get murdered before I ever got a fair trial." He grabbed his phone. "I know we need to call the cops, but we *really* need to talk to Connor first." He tapped the screen a couple of times, and then Naomi could hear a ringing sound. Jared shoved the phone into her hand. "Here, you tell him what happened. My head is still spinning—you can do a better job of explaining it."

Before she could respond, she heard a faint click and then a voice she hadn't heard in nearly twenty years. "Jared, where are you, buddy? I've been looking for you."

Naomi's heart shattered like glass. Old memories began to spring to life in the back of her mind. Images of herself and Connor Ryan as husband and wife. They'd practically been kids back then. Barely old enough to legally be married. She nervously cleared her throat. "Actually, it's me," she said. And then, when he didn't respond for a few moments, she added, "It's Naomi."

"I know," he said, his tone sounding oddly flat. "I remember your voice."

Bounty hunter Connor Ryan had been literally gut punched several times in his life. He knew exactly how it felt. A burst of pain, followed by breathlessness. And that's how he felt right now, hearing his former wife's voice after all these years.

Of course he'd known that she'd moved back to town. But he'd gone out of his way to avoid her. Had planned to spend the rest of his life avoiding her.

"There's been a shooting," Naomi said, and he clung to her words like a lifeline, grateful for the chance to focus his attention back on the job and away from his emotions. "A man is dead," she added.

"Are you and Jared all right? Where are you? Are you together?"

"Two gunmen are after us. We're at the Lexford Sawmill. These two guys, they killed a man and framed Jared. I saw it happen. I saw them force a gun into Jared's hand and fire it."

"I'm on my way."

"No! I don't want you to get hurt. I just want you to call the cops, tell them what happened. They should know what situation they'll be walking into."

"You know that they'll need to take Jared into custody," Connor warned her.

"Honestly, I'd be thrilled to have him in police custody right now," she replied. "He'd be safer there than he is here. The police just need to know that there's more to the situation than is obvious on the surface. I don't know yet why Jared missed his court date but he obviously wasn't trying to skip town. Make sure the authorities know that and maybe the magistrate will consider bail for him if he's charged with murder. Maybe you'll be able to bond him out. It's worth a try." She took an audible breath. "In the meantime, I don't have the address of the house where the shooting happened, but it's blue and white and it's on the side of the river down here by the sawmill. The poor man's body is on the back patio."

Dread and sorrow formed a hard knot in the center of Connor's chest. "That's Kevin Ashton's place. He's a friend."

"I'm sorry," Naomi said softly.

"What does the killer look like?" Connor asked a few moments later as he pulled up in front of Kevin's house. He'd already been in the area, driving around where Jared was known to hang out. Jared was a nice guy, but he'd forfeited his bond when he'd skipped his court appointment earlier in the day and as his bail bondsman, it was Connor's job to find him and bring him in.

Connor climbed out of his truck and jogged around to the back of the house, steeling himself for what he might find. He hoped that Naomi was wrong and that Kevin was still alive. When he saw his friend, the catastrophic injuries from the gunshots were obvious. He reached for Kevin's neck, hoping against reason that he would find a pulse. But the second he touched him, there was absolutely no doubt that his friend was gone. "God bless and keep you," he prayed quietly. He hated leaving his friend out here like this, and wanted to at least carry his body inside the house. But he knew that for the sake of the police investigation he needed to leave things as they were.

He'd kept the phone connection with Naomi open, so of course she'd heard him. "I'm so sorry," she said again.

"You said someone killed Kevin, framed Jared for it, and now they're coming after you and Jared?"

"Yes."

"You're still at the sawmill?" He glanced around, saw the broken branches in some of the surrounding bushes, and realized Naomi and Jared had made their way across the connecting lawns to get to the sawmill.

"Yes, we're still here."

"I'm going to call the police while I head over there. I want you to silence Jared's phone but keep an eye on the screen. I'll call you right back."

"No, wait—"

"Bye." Connor disconnected, called 9-1-1 and reported the situation all while getting back to his truck and driving to the end of the road.

When he arrived at the sawmill, he killed the truck's lights and the engine and listened for anything moving in the quiet. The caretakers of the sawmill property kept a few exterior light fixtures working, but kids came out here to throw rocks and break the bulbs each time they were replaced. Connor had done exactly that when he was an obnoxious kid back in the day. Sometimes Naomi had been with him.

She knew the place well and she'd sounded calm and fairly confident that she was safe when he'd talked with her. Connor's original instinct had been to go straight to Naomi wherever she and Jared were hiding. But now it seemed like a better idea to take advantage of the darkness and hunt the bad guys. For the sake of Naomi's and Jared's safety he could hope that the criminals had already given up on finding them and had taken off, but he couldn't count on that.

Meanwhile, maybe when the cops rolled up

they wouldn't mistake Connor for the killer and open fire on him.

Careful to dim the light and sound from his phone, he crept into the forested area of the property and called Jared's phone.

"They're in here." Naomi's whispered words when she answered sent a chill through his bones. "The killers."

"Where?" Connor asked.

"The admin building. Do you remember the pantry in the lunchroom?"

She was trying so hard to be quiet that he could barely make out her words. And she sounded terrified.

The old protective instinct when it came to Naomi roared to life. "I'll be right there."

He changed course so that he was moving in her direction. The admin building was tucked away in a corner of the sprawling sawmill site. If the gunmen were searching all the buildings, there was no way they would have gotten to that one so fast. The fact that the thugs were already so close to finding her told Connor a couple of things. They had decent tracking skills and they hadn't given up and run away when things went sideways, so they were likely professionals. And they were familiar enough with the grounds of the sawmill to quickly locate buildings where someone might try to hide, which meant they were possibly locals.

Since the sawmill had fallen into disrepair decades ago, many of the windows were broken as were locks on the doors that were still standing. There wasn't much of real value left inside, and the buildings had all taken a fair amount of storm damage over the years, leaving some of the structures barely standing. The admin building was probably the one in the best shape. It had been a smart choice on Naomi's part to hide in because the sturdy walls meant it was more secure. But if the gunmen were already inside…she'd have a harder time getting away from them.

Connor found the front door of the admin building slightly ajar. He pushed it further open and walked in.

There were offices on the left side of the ground floor of the building as well as the second floor. The right side of the ground floor used to house a kitchen and dining room. Connor stood still in the darkness and listened carefully. He could hear two people walking briskly on the old wooden and tile floors, shoving some of the dusty old furniture aside and occasionally opening and shutting interior doors. Must be the thugs.

Determined not to draw attention to himself, Connor stepped back outside and went to the rear of the building, where he found a broken window leading into the kitchen. "I'm almost there," he whispered into his phone. "Is the interior door to the pantry still in place?"

"Yes," Naomi whispered. "I closed it. We're behind it."

"When you hear three taps, that will be me." Once he was inside the building he wanted to avoid talking as much as possible. Random sounds could be brushed off as nothing concerning by the assailants. But if the thugs heard a human voice, he and Naomi and Jared would be in trouble.

Connor climbed in the kitchen window directly over the sink. He dropped to the floor and made his way to the pantry door, where he tapped three times.

The door opened slowly. Although the ambient light was faint, he could still see Naomi's face.

He had seen her picture recently. She'd been in the news as a local hero when she'd moved back to town and invested in a local furniture factory on the verge of declaring bankruptcy, saving the jobs of all the people who worked there. She didn't look much different from back in the day, really. A little heavier, as was he. There were a few new lines marking the passage of time around the outer corners of her eyes and around the edges of her mouth, as was also the case for him. And she'd taken to wearing glasses. Something Connor occasionally did when he had a lot of reading to do.

In her presence, he felt an almost elemental connection to her. Like the feeling he'd had when they were married. Before he could think of anything to say, the sound of footsteps coming down the hallway and into the connecting dining room refocused his attention back to the need to get Naomi to safety.

Gesturing for her and her brother to follow him, Connor headed back to the kitchen and the window above the sink. He gestured at Naomi to climb out first, and then took hold of her arm to help her, grateful that all the glass around the frame had long since been cleared away so she wouldn't get cut. He noticed a tear in her jacket near her shoulder, and a smear of dried blood. She'd been injured. Had she been shot?

Once she was outside, Connor gestured for Jared to go out the window next. Something seemed to be off with Jared's balance, and after pushing through the window he landed on his hip instead of his feet and let out a loud yelp. The sound of running footsteps in the dining room immediately followed. The bad guys had heard him and seemed to be heading for the exit to intercept them.

Connor quickly leaped out the window, determined to hustle Jared and Naomi out of the way before the gunmen could find them. But he was too late.

A dark-haired man ran around the corner, gun drawn, but the guy stopped short and appeared surprised to see Connor.

Connor moved for his own weapon, but before he could reach it the assailant took aim.

Naomi, who'd stepped back into the forest shadows when she first cleared the window, now lurched forward, shoving at the gunman's arm, causing him to fire wildly into the sky.

Connor grabbed the opportunity she'd given him and threw a punch that connected with the thug's jaw.

The man's gun flew out of his hand as he fell.

Before Connor could grab him and cuff him, the attacker was back on his feet. He glared at Connor, and began to circle him. But then he was distracted by the sound of approaching sirens.

From somewhere in the dark a man's voice, presumably the criminal's accomplice, shouted, "Let's go!"

The thug in front of Connor cast a scowl toward Naomi, letting it linger for a moment in a way that set off warning alarms in the pit of Connor's stomach.

And then the creep turned and ran off into the darkness.

TWO

"Get ready to put your hands up when the cops get closer," Connor said as he took a couple of steps away from Naomi.

She watched him pull the handgun from the holster at his hip and set it on the ground. Then he reached down and pulled a smaller gun from inside the calf of his boot and set that on the ground, too.

"With officers rolling up on a scene in response to a reported homicide, it's best not to give them any reason to overreact."

"That's the truth," Jared said from the spot a little deeper in the surrounding forest.

"How exactly did all this start?" Naomi asked her brother while keeping an eye on Connor as he returned to stand about an arm's length away from her. "How did you end up at Kevin's house?"

While waiting for him to reply she noticed that Connor kept his gaze moving, turning his head slightly to watch their surroundings as if he thought the criminals might return to stage another attack. That didn't seem likely given the arrival of the police, but maybe Connor knew something she didn't.

After all, he was a bounty hunter now. She'd known that before tonight, but it was still a mind-boggling reality considering the fact that he'd been a petty thief back when they were teenagers. At the time he'd been no fan of law enforcement.

It felt unreal to be standing beside him. She kept her gaze on her former husband while waiting for her brother's response. What had Connor's life been like for the last couple of decades? Did she even know the man he was now?

"I was at home, after work, feeling kind of restless and lonesome and like I'd never get things right," Jared finally began, having apparently finally organized his thoughts. "And I figured I'd just head on down to Indigo Street and see what was going on."

"Why didn't you show up for your court appointment at two o'clock?" Connor interjected.

"I got mixed-up on the date," Jared said, self-disgust evident in his tone.

Naomi felt a slow roll of frustration and defensiveness on his behalf. He had dyslexia, which carried with it a tendency to sometimes have trouble keeping dates and times and appointments straight.

"I had my phone turned off and charging for a while. By the time I turned it back on and got your and Connor's messages about missing the appointment, it was too late to get it straightened out today," Jared continued, directing his response to his sister. "The courthouse was closed, so I'd planned on being down there first thing tomorrow morning."

Connor cleared his throat. "You should have called my office as soon as you got the messages."

Jared just fidgeted, clearly having no response to that. With a sigh, Naomi moved on to her next questions. "What happened after you got to Indigo Street? Did you hit the bars?" Naomi fought to keep the disappointment from her voice. Jared had been through enough trauma tonight. He didn't need her adding to it.

"I was almost inside Club Sapphire when I realized what I was doing. I was angry at myself and sad and that combination had me heading to get a drink without consciously making that decision. But then it hit me, that drinking wasn't what I wanted to do. I didn't want to throw away four months of sobriety. So I called Kevin."

"And he invited you to his house?"

"No. He was at the coffee shop I told you about. Coffee Bean Arena. I know I've mentioned it to you before. It's a good place to hang out when you're trying to stay sober."

That's right, she *did* remember him talking about some friends he'd made there. Both employees and patrons, if she remembered correctly.

A police cruiser came into view, blue lights flashing. A bright spotlight shone on the forest, moving around as if searching. It reminded Naomi that anyone could be hiding in the surrounding woods. Connor was right to remain vigilant. The gunmen could be watching the three of them right now. Even with the cops nearby, the bad guys could still fire off some more shots while their targets were standing still and then slip away.

"Kevin spent a lot of time in that coffee shop," Jared continued, his voice shaking, obviously fighting back tears. "He met a lot of people there trying to stay sober. Those two *killers* pretended they'd shown up for that reason. Claimed they needed to talk, but a folk singer started up on that small stage and you couldn't really hear so Kevin invited us to hang out and talk in his backyard. When we got there he went in the house and came out a short time later with a pot of coffee and some cups. He put them on the table, but we didn't sit down right away. The guys wanted to walk around the property, checking out the view of the river. Eventually, we came back to the patio and sat down. I drank a cup of coffee that someone had already poured into a mug. And then I got dizzy. That's when I called you."

"And shortly after that is when I showed up and saw the two thugs frame you for murder," Naomi said dully.

The police car was drawing nearer. Farther back, a second patrol car had pulled onto the property.

The cops' searchlight moved closer toward them. Naomi felt herself growing nervous even though she knew she hadn't done anything wrong.

"They're going to think I did it." Jared's voice sounded faint, like he'd given up hope. "I can't let them lock me up."

"If they arrest you I'll do everything I can to bond you out of jail as quickly as possible," Connor said.

The calm and certain tone of his voice made Naomi feel a little better.

And then the glaring searchlight settled on them, so bright it felt like a blinding assault.

"Put your hands up." The commanding voice came out through the rooftop speaker. "Stay where you are. Don't move."

"Easy," Connor said quietly to Naomi and Jared.

Naomi took a deep breath and tried to calm her hammering heart.

The officers approached cautiously. When they were just a few feet away, one of them broke into a slight smile. "You out here chasing down thugs tonight, Connor?"

"You could say that."

"Go ahead and put your hands down," the cop said.

Naomi dropped her hands. "Don't worry, we'll get this straightened out," she said to Jared. She turned toward her brother, but he was gone.

"Was that Jared Santelli? Did your bail jumper commit a homicide and then get away?" Detective Romanov of the Range River Police Department glared at Connor. "Why didn't you cuff him when you found him instead of leaving him free to run away?"

"The situation is more complicated than that." Connor held the detective's angry gaze, trying to radiate calm to keep the situation from escalating. He and his team had put forth a lot of effort into convincing her to trust them and their efforts to help keep Range River safe. For the bounty hunters to do their jobs as quickly and efficiently as possible they needed a good working relationship with the police. He could only hope this latest incident wouldn't mess up the tentative truce they'd managed to build.

"You've got that right, it *is* complicated," the detective said crisply. "Right now I've got a couple of detectives initiating a murder investigation in a backyard a short distance away from here and I've got a record of you calling it in."

Officers were already moving through the nearby woods and the interior of the sawmill's administration building, searching for any sign of the two gunmen or Jared.

"My brother didn't kill anyone." Naomi stepped forward.

"Jared Santelli is your brother?"

"Yes. My name's Naomi Pearson."

"Okay, Naomi, tell me about your brother. Better yet, call him and get him to come back here and talk to me."

"You don't understand." Naomi shook her head. "You need to catch the actual killers, first."

Connor listened as she laid out everything she'd witnessed, from beginning to end. Her voice was shaky, but her explanation was clear and focused. That clearheadedness was something he'd always admired about her. It had given him a sense of calm when they were younger and she was his refuge from his chaotic alcoholic homelife. Her own family was just as bad, which made it all the more amazing that she'd been able to hold herself together.

Until she hadn't been.

Maybe that was why it felt so especially heartbreaking later when she lost that clearheadedness right when they both needed it most—when they were forced to face a painful tragedy together. She'd tossed aside reason and taken a deep dive into anger and blame instead.

The memory caught him up short and he took a deep, steadying breath. Much as he wanted to leave that part of his life behind, he couldn't seem to shake it. Even after all this time. Their marriage had crashed and burned, ripped apart by grief, triggered by a sad event that he carried as a weight on his heart every single day. One that he'd kept secret from the younger siblings he worked with as well as his close friends. Only Naomi had known what he was going through—but he hadn't been able to turn to her for comfort as her own pain had opened a chasm between them.

In the end, Naomi had been the one to call it quits for their marriage. She was the one who'd said she thought it would be best for them to go their separate ways. What could he do but grant her that wish? So they'd gotten a divorce.

Things were over between the two of them a long time ago. What he felt for her now was... confusing. He couldn't just turn off the emotion he'd felt flare back to life when he'd first heard her voice over Jared's phone. But they were way beyond being able to ever pick up where they'd left off.

In the years they'd been apart he'd built the stable life he'd always wanted. With the help of the younger siblings he'd adopted and raised after their parents died, he'd formed Range River Bail Bonds both to protect the community from crime and to offer a helping hand to people who'd been as misguided as he'd once been. It had been his motivation to help Naomi's brother.

He'd moved on. He did not want or need Naomi anymore.

Of course he would help Jared because that was his job. But that was all he would do.

"Call your brother right now," the detective said when Naomi finished her account. "Tell him to come back. We need to talk. Most especially, we need him to help us identify the two gunmen."

At that point a uniformed officer stepped up, caught the detective's attention and shook his head. Connor took that to mean the cops searching the buildings and surrounding area hadn't found any trace of the three men who had fled the scene.

"So you believe me?" Naomi said hopefully, drawing Romanov's attention back to her.

"I'm keeping an open mind." The detective glanced at Connor. "Meanwhile, Jared did violate his bond and he needs to face a magistrate to sort that out. Possibly Connor can issue a new bond."

"It would be best to get him to turn himself in," Connor said to Naomi. "Especially with the gunmen still at large. They might try to get to him before I do."

Connor could see her eyes widen in fear before she grabbed the phone from her pocket, her face falling when her call went to Jared's voice mail. *"Call me, now,"* she said forcefully into the phone after the beep. "I mean it."

Her voice broke on the last two words. As she turned slightly and wiped at her eyes, Connor spotted a torn spot and dried blood on her jacket and remembered noticing her injury. "We need an ambulance for her," he said to Romanov.

Naomi turned toward him. "For me?" She shook her head. "It doesn't feel like I got shot. I think I just got grazed by some kind of fragment."

She pulled off her jacket.

"I think you're right," Romanov said, leaning over beside Connor to take a look at what appeared to be a deep scratch on her injured shoulder. "But I can still get EMS here if you want."

Naomi shook her head. "I don't need them."

"Do you want us to go to Kevin's house with you?" Connor asked the detective. "To answer questions or expand on our statements?"

"The last thing I need is extra people tromping around on my murder scene. There is one thing I do want to get clear before I go. I'm assuming you would have said something if either of the gunmen looked familiar to you. Is that correct?"

"Yes, ma'am, that is correct," Connor confirmed.

She turned to Naomi. "Have you ever seen either of them before?"

Naomi shook her head.

"I'll have some mug shots for you to look at tomorrow."

"They seemed like professionals," Connor added. "And they said and did some things that made it appear as if they were specifically after Naomi." He shook his head. "I don't think this is just about Jared."

The detective arched an eyebrow at Naomi. "It sounds like you need to be very, very careful." She turned to Connor. "While you're hunting for Jared, if you come across any information about the shooters you let me know. Immediately."

"The way bounty hunting generally works is that the cops use their technology, and all the records they have access to, to track down people while I use different resources."

"Different resources?" Naomi asked.

"Yeah, more along the lines of digging into the fugitive's personal connections, habits.

Sometimes there's information I can get from paid confidential informants." Connor turned to Naomi. She was sitting beside him in his pickup as he drove her back to her car. He'd been able to convince her that she'd be better off not driving until her emotions had time to settle, but she needed to pick up her purse.

"Jared." Naomi turned to Connor. "The *fugitive* you referred to is named Jared."

"Right." He'd been unintentionally insensitive. Not exactly unusual for him. Naomi used to be understanding of his awkwardness, knowing that it never stemmed from malice. She always seemed to understand what he was really trying to say, even when he bungled the delivery…right up until she stopped trying to understand him at all.

Whatever. They weren't on a date right now and he didn't need to win her over. He didn't *want* to win her over.

He cleared his throat and offered the same response he gave to all of his clients if they got touchy while he was trying to do his job. "This isn't personal. It's not my intention to be offensive, but I'm not out looking for your brother. I'm hunting a fugitive *who happens to be* your brother. And considering that he's been framed for murder, and you've apparently been targeted as well, I don't have time to walk on eggshells. If you get offended by what I do or say, that's your choice."

She began to blink rapidly, unsuccessfully holding back tears.

"I know you're worried about him and you're scared," Connor said more gently. "But I am going to do my best to find him."

"Thank you." She wiped away the tears with the backs of her hands and straightened her glasses.

"I want to ask you a few questions right now so that I can plan what I need to do next."

She lifted an eyebrow. In the old days, that would have been the signal for an argument. So Connor was relieved when she simply said, "Okay. What's your first question?"

"The cops are going to do all the obvious stuff like post officers at his apartment, put alerts on his debit or credit cards, and try find his location through his phone. They've probably already staked out his car, waiting for him to show up there."

"It seems wrong to me that they'd be putting so much energy into looking for him instead of the actual bad guys."

"They'll be looking for all three of them— but he's the only one *I* can legally track down and apprehend because of his violated bond status." Connor made a point of looking directly at Naomi. "When I find him I will take him into custody. And then we'll figure things out from there."

She nodded. "I understand."

"If he really is committed to going on the run, I think he's smart enough to stay away from his car and to avoid using his phone or credit cards. So, for at least the next few hours he'll probably be nearby. I already know he likes Club Sapphire because he's mentioned it to me. What other bars does he hang out at?"

"He told me he doesn't hang out at bars anymore. He's done with that."

Maybe that was true. Or maybe—more likely—Jared wished it was true, but he was, in fact, lying to his sister.

"Okay, where did he used to hang out? He's probably still got friends there and somebody whose reasoning is impaired by alcohol is more likely to help a fugitive."

"I honestly don't know. I wasn't here for... for the worst of it. By the time I'd gotten back, he'd already been scared straight by that arrest."

Connor nodded, remembering how shaken Jared had been when he and his friends had gotten busted for drug trafficking. By all accounts, Jared wasn't a dealer himself, but he'd been hanging out with his dealer friends in the wrong place at the wrong time. Maybe it really had been a wake-up call to get his act together—one that Jared badly needed.

"I just moved back two months ago and during all that time he's been walking a straight line," Naomi continued.

"What about you? What have you been up to lately?"

Naomi drew herself up, appearing offended. "What are you talking about?"

"I'm just trying to look at this from every angle. Why might those thugs have targeted Jared *and you*?"

"Seriously? Are you insinuating that I've been doing something illegal? *Me?*"

Connor took a deep breath and tried to hold on to his temper. They'd never get anywhere if they let this fall into one of their epic fights. "I'm not insinuating anything. I'm asking. So that I can do my job and find your brother. Before anyone else does. Maybe even help find the shooters, too. And the fact is, I don't know you at all." *Not anymore.* "Tell me about your life. A brief history. Humor me."

After a moment she shook her head and

visibly relaxed a little. "After…after I left, I wanted to start fresh so I moved with my aunt and uncle to Las Vegas. Eventually I met a nice man there. A good, Christian man. His name was Matt Pearson. I became a Christian, as well." Her voice grew husky and she wiped away tears. "We got married. He'd started a business with his brothers and it did very well. He passed away two years ago." She paused and took a deep breath.

"I'm sorry to hear that," Connor said.

She nodded. "Thank you. I helped run the business and I learned a lot. But after my husband passed away my heart wasn't in it anymore and I sold my interest to my brothers-in-law."

"Why did you decide to come back to Range River?"

"I'd kept in touch with some of my cousins over the years. I knew Jared was having a tough time and I learned that the Stuart Furniture Company was about to get shuttered, putting a lot of people out of work. I had money to invest, so I approached the owner, bought the company and moved back. I don't know much about furniture but I do know how to manage a manufacturing facility." She held up her hands. "That's it. That's the whole story."

"So there haven't been any threats on your life before tonight?"

"No."

"No animosity connected to your new business or the old one?"

"Not at all." She shook her head and glanced out the side window.

Was she hiding something? Connor waited a moment to see if she would add anything, but she didn't.

He pulled up close to Naomi's parked car and stopped. "Wait here while I grab your purse for you. Then, after I drive you home, I'll come back and take a quick look around at Club Sapphire."

"I'm going with you while you look for Jared."

Connor shook his head. "I don't think that's a good idea."

"Listen, if Jared sees the cops—or you—he's going to run. Imagine what's going through his mind. His friend was murdered right in front of him. He was framed for it. And then he was chased and shot at." She shook her head. "He's not thinking clearly—but I know I can get through to him. Convince him that he needs to turn himself in." She paused. "Now that I think about it, maybe things will go better if I look for him in the club without you."

She moved to grab the door handle.

"Wait." He reached over to place a hand on her arm. "What about your own safety?"

She held his gaze for a moment. "I'm not blind to the danger, Connor. Honestly, I'm terrified. But I can't just abandon my brother." She looked down for a moment. "And maybe I'm selfish, too. I want to talk to him. Just the two of us. Before cops or bounty hunters or anyone else is involved. That way, I can find out if there's anything else he knows that he's kept hidden."

She made a solid argument.

Connor tilted his head back slightly, offering up a prayer for guidance, wisdom and protection for himself and Naomi. "All right," he finally said. "We'll go together so I can make sure you're safe, but I'll let you take the lead—and if we do find him, I'll give you space to talk. For now, let's go have a look around. I know a couple of the bartenders at Club Sapphire, maybe one of them has seen him tonight."

They got out of the truck. Connor caught her gaze and held it. "Stay close to me and pay attention to everything going on around you."

"I will."

Clouds had rolled into town over the last hour. They'd dropped down low and a light rain was starting to fall. Connor glanced around, trying to discern if they were being watched, but the roughening weather made that hard to do. He stuck by Naomi's side as they headed toward the nightclub.

He hoped that the gunmen were long gone from the area, focused on evading the police. But he feared that, since they seemed to be professionals, they would continue to hang around to finish their job. And doing that clearly involved harm to Naomi.

His first step would be to find his fugitive, hopefully inside Club Sapphire. Then maybe Jared could give them information that would help keep Naomi safe. She wasn't his client, and she hadn't been his wife for a long time, but he still felt the pull of responsibility for her protection. Especially with someone intent on seeing her dead.

THREE

Loud music inside the nightclub vibrated in the pit of Naomi's stomach as lights in gradient shades from blue to purple pulsed around the edge of the dance floor.

Connor remained close by her side as they walked around the perimeter of the crowded club. "I doubt Jared would be on the dance floor." He leaned close enough for Naomi to feel his breath on her ear as he spoke. Even so, she had to concentrate to make sense of his words in the midst of the continuing waves of sound. "We'll check the tables first," he added. "If we don't see him there we'll check at the bar and see if one of the bartenders knows anything."

"Okay."

Naomi occasionally glanced toward the dance floor as they walked, but mainly she kept her attention on the patrons sunk into the club chairs arranged around low tables. The first time someone glanced back in her direction as she walked by, she was struck by the uneasy realization that she and Connor might not be the only people in here looking for Jared. The bad guys could be here searching for him, and keeping an eye out for her, too.

A cold wave of apprehension passed through her at the thought, and she wrapped her rain-dampened coat a little tighter around her body. It didn't alleviate the chill. She began to tremble.

Dear Lord, please protect and help Connor and me. And protect Jared, too. Her fear for Jared was stronger than her fear for herself. Her brother was the one who'd been framed for murder and was now on the run, terrified and alone. Naomi at least had someone to help her. The fact that it was her ex-husband was still a little hard to reckon with.

She'd known that Connor was a bounty hunter, but seeing him right now, confidently doing a job that regularly put him in harm's way, was unsettling. So was the fact that the years had been so kind to him. Of course he looked older with the effects of life experience etched on his face. She had noticed a slight scar bisecting his left eyebrow and another scar on his chin. None of it made him look any less handsome.

She shook off her musings, determined to be attentive to her surroundings. Her life could depend on it.

They made their way to the back of the club, up a short set of stairs to an elevated platform where patrons could get a better view of the dance floor. Still no sign of Jared or the gunmen. Connor remained close, frequently glancing at her as if to make certain she was still there. The feelings and memories his protective behavior brought up were reassuring and unsettling at the same time.

They continued walking until they finally came to the bar, where Connor waved over a bartender.

"Hey, Connor, how are you doing?" The bartender slid a couple of coasters in front of Connor and Naomi. "What are you drinking?"

"Actually, we're here for information."

"Of course." The bartender, a man with a shaved head and a beard, nodded. "What do you need to know?"

"Have you seen Jared Santelli in here tonight?"

He shook his head. "I've been here since four o'clock and I haven't seen him."

The bartender knew Jared by name? That was concerning. Naomi got out her phone, pulled up a picture and showed it to him, just to be certain they were talking about the same man.

The bartender glanced at the screen then smiled and nodded. "Yeah, that's Jared. Nice guy. Is he okay?"

"Have you seen him at all recently?" Naomi asked, fearful of the answer. Maybe her brother wasn't doing as well in the battle with his drinking problem as he'd led her to believe.

"It's been a while since I've seen him, actually. I used to see him every weekend."

"Who'd he hang around with when he was here?" Connor asked.

The bartender shrugged. "Other regulars, if they were here. If not, he'd just keep to himself. He was chill. He just sat and drank. Never bothered anybody."

"We're also looking for a couple of professional thugs," Connor added. He gave a brief description of the gunmen.

The bartender's eyes narrowed. "Sounds like a couple of guys who came in last night. You do this job for a while and you get good at recognizing trouble when it walks in the door. These guys had that look." He ran his hand over his beard. "They sat at the bar and kept an eye on the door most of the time. They didn't drink much. They were obviously look-ing for somebody."

A chill ran up Naomi's spine and she re-flexively turned around to see if anyone in the nightclub was watching her. Those murderers had been right here just last night, looking for Jared probably. Maybe they were here now. She and Connor could have missed them. Even with the lights flashing on the dance floor and the small lanterns on the tables, it was hard to get a clear view of anyone's face.

"I assume they paid cash," Connor said. "No credit card receipt."

"That's right."

"Could I get a look at your security video?"

The bartender shook his head and offered a rueful smile. "Sorry, but the answer's the same as it always is. I want to help you catch bad guys, but the owner is committed to protect-ing the patrons' privacy. He won't turn over that footage without a warrant."

"But that makes no sense." Naomi couldn't hold back. "Don't the people who come here value their safety?"

The bartender lifted his eyebrows slightly. "People have all kinds of priorities. And their top priority isn't always good. Or wise."

Disappointment took hold of Naomi as she considered the truth of what he said.

Connor thanked the bartender and slid some cash across the bar toward him. "Thanks."

The bartender pocketed the money. "If I see Jared, or if the two guys I was telling you about show up again, I'll call you."

"Appreciate it." Connor turned to Naomi. "Before we go, I need to text Detective Romanov and tell her what we learned here."

Moments later, after the message was sent, they reached the exit. Connor stood in the doorway directly in front of Naomi while he scanned the area outside.

"Okay," he finally said, stepping aside so she could walk through the door. "Let's get you home."

"Actually, I have an idea for another place to check."

"Another bar?"

She shook her head. "I was thinking of Coffee Bean Arena." The trendy coffee shop was situated right in the center of the pedestrian mall. "It's where Jared said he was meeting with Kevin Ashton when the thugs found him."

"Good idea, let's go."

They crossed the street and walked toward the coffee shop, rain still falling steadily. Naomi pulled up the hood on her jacket. She smelled the rich scent of espresso from several yards away.

The interior of the coffee shop was a sharp contrast to the nightclub, with gentle light throughout and an upbeat buzz of conversation interspersed with occasional laughter. Naomi made a quick scan of the area, but she didn't see her brother. "I'm going to try again to call him," she said. As before, his phone rang several times and then went to voice mail. "I'm at the Coffee Bean Arena," she said after the tone. "Where are you? Call me! Now. *Please.*"

As she disconnected Connor gave her a sharp look. "If the thugs have caught him and have his phone, now they know exactly where *you* are."

She shrugged. The thought that Connor might be right scared her, but she would do everything she could think of to find Jared, nevertheless. Besides, it wasn't like she could retract the message now that she'd left it.

They got in line at the front counter.

"Do you know a man named Jared Santelli?" Connor asked the guy taking coffee orders. "We need to find him."

"Sorry, no."

Naomi held up her phone where she still

had his photo pulled up to show the cashier. "This is him. He's my brother and we're trying to help him."

The guy shook his head.

She was surprised since Jared had told her that he had friends he saw here regularly. "He's mentioned someone named Anjelica—she works here, right? Is she here now?"

The guy glanced over at a raven-haired woman behind the bakery case. "Anjelica. You got a minute?"

Naomi nodded to the man. "Thank you."

When Anjelica approached, Naomi introduced herself and Connor, and then held up her phone with Jared's photo visible. "My brother is missing. His name's Jared. Have you seen him?"

"Jared's missing?" The woman's friendly smile quickly vanished. "What happened?" She stepped around the counter and the three of them moved toward the nearby tables.

"He's in danger," Naomi said, choking up a little and fighting to hold back tears as she said the words. "We're looking for him. The police are looking for him, too. I believe he was here late this afternoon."

Anjelica nodded. "Yes. He was here with Kevin Ashton—and then they started talking to a couple of other men I've never seen before. Kevin was always meeting people here to help them. Maybe you should talk to him. I have his number if you want it."

The image of Kevin's lifeless body on the patio behind his house pushed its way into Naomi's mind. Sorrow, heavy in her chest and stomach, made it impossible for her to form the words to tell the young woman what had happened to him.

"Let's sit down," Connor said gently.

Naomi headed for the closest table, in front of the window.

"Not by the window," Connor said with a shake of his head.

Of course. Naomi was a target for danger, just like her brother.

Connor led the way to a table in the back, in a relatively quiet corner. When they were all seated, he told Anjelica that Kevin had been shot and killed, leaving out the graphic details.

She gasped and tears rolled down her face. "No," she said, shaking her head. "Not Kevin. He was such a good man. He helped people. He helped so many people trying to kick addictions."

Connor lightly laid a hand on her shoulder. "Can I pray for you?"

Naomi's jaw dropped a little. Connor was a *praying* man now?

"Yes, please."

Naomi quickly recovered herself and laid a hand on the woman's shoulder, joining in the prayer.

A couple of employees watched them from a distance and made their way over. Anjelica told them what had happened and they both teared up, too.

"My brother was with Kevin when it happened," Naomi said softly. "Now he's in danger of being murdered by the same men."

She showed the other employees the picture of her brother and they promised to contact her if he came into the coffee shop. She gave them her number, and then Connor handed out business cards with his number on it. "Call the police first if you actually see him," Connor told them. "They can respond the fastest and make sure he's safe. But call me first if you hear something that might help us locate him."

When they were ready to leave, Connor again took a look outside first to make sure it was safe. Despite the rain, there were a lot of people on the pedestrian thoroughfare. As the people passed by wearing hats and jackets with the collar flipped up to ward off the weather,

Naomi could only see a little bit of their faces. If Kevin's killers were watching her right now, maybe even getting ready to take a shot, would she recognize them? Probably not.

The temperature was plummeting and Connor noticed rivulets with bits of ice rolling down the windshield as he started up his truck and scanned the parking lot around them. He cranked up the heater in case Naomi was cold. He'd seen her hugging herself a lot since the moment he'd caught up with her and Jared at the sawmill. That could be due to temperature or it could be due to trauma. Or both.

"Let's get you home," he said. "Where do you live?"

"No," she said, shaking her head. "We can't give up looking for Jared already. It's not that late. We could check a few other places."

"I'm not giving up. After I get you home, I'm going back out to search for him. But the places where I plan to go, you would be more of a distraction than a help." Connor had several paid informants in town and wanted to find out what they had to say. If there were professional hit men milling around Range River, especially around the trendy hub of Indigo Street, people who lived and moved on the shadowy side of things would know all about it. But they tended to clam up around strangers.

"I don't mean to insult you," he added. "But I can visit more places and get more things done tonight if I'm alone."

"I understand," she said. "And I definitely want you to get results."

She pulled out her phone to make a call. Connor could hear the connection to Jared's outgoing voice mail message. "Please call me. I want to help you. I'll do everything I can." She broke down into tears and disconnected.

Connor's heart ached for her. He didn't want to imagine how he'd feel if he were in her situation and one of his own siblings was in grave danger. He was determined to do everything he could to find Jared. And he would do everything he could to protect Naomi. At the moment he was worried that she wasn't as concerned about potential further attacks against herself as she ought to be.

"Instead of staying at home alone, why don't you let me drop you off at a friend's house?" he offered. He figured if she didn't live alone, now was the time she would tell him. "Or maybe you could stay with relatives tonight. This is a tough time for you to be by yourself. And there's safety in numbers."

He thought about offering to take her to his own home, a historical inn on the edge of the river that he'd turned into a private residence. He could call in family and friends, people connected with his bail bonds company, to help protect her. He had a few dogs who would give an alert if prowlers showed up on the property, as well.

But something held him back from making that offer. He could admit to himself that maybe it had to do with the confusion of feelings Naomi had triggered in him. Some part of him thought an invitation for her to stay with him would not be wise.

"I'll be okay," Naomi said, hugging herself again. "If I can't go look for Jared then I just want to go home." She turned toward him. "I'm living on the southeastern edge of Wolf Lake these days. In the Granite Bay area."

"Granite Bay?"

Naomi managed a faint smile. "I've come a long way since we were kids." She sighed. "My husband and I built up a strong business together and I'm financially comfortable, which is nice. More important than that, after spending time with him I found faith. That's what changed everything. Made life bearable." She brushed her hair out of her eyes. "I know the value of peace of mind is far greater than any monetary prize. As is the value of hope. And healing." She glanced at him. "Especially healing."

Even though she didn't say it, he felt certain he knew what she was referring to. The heartbreaking event that tore them apart all those years ago. The loss of their unborn child shortly after Naomi's third month of pregnancy, just when everyone said it was safe to get their hopes up.

And they *had* gotten their hopes up. As soon as Naomi discovered she was pregnant, they'd gotten married. She was eighteen and he was nineteen. They'd given in to fanciful dreams about the family they would build. The love they would share and the fun they would have.

And then, without warning, that dream was gone. Both of them were so young. The sorrow and confusion tore them apart. Following the advice of Naomi's mother, they'd been waiting for the three-month mark to announce their good news. Connor was planning to tell his family and friends right at the time they lost the baby. Afterward, he found he couldn't talk about it. Not even with the younger siblings that Connor eventually adopted and raised. They knew he'd been married a long time ago.

And that he'd gotten divorced. And that was all they knew.

Connor forced himself to settle his thoughts back on the here and now as he kept an eye out for any approaching threats. He finally pulled out of the parking lot and headed in the direction of Wolf Lake and Granite Bay.

He didn't speak for a few minutes because the only thing he could think about was the misery of that loss—and he was absolutely not going to have *that* conversation with her. Not after all these years.

"Some context could help me locate Jared," he finally said. "What's been going on in his life lately besides the stuff I already know about? Who might he have made angry? Who would want to see him sent away to prison for life on murder charges? Or see him dead?"

Naomi shook her head. "I can't think of anything. He's been doing his best to stay out of trouble since he got arrested. Working on getting himself sober and together."

"Maybe it's something he's *stopped* doing that somebody has a problem with. Any ideas on that?"

She shrugged and turned to him. "You'd know better than me. You're the one who's bailed him out of trouble on and off over the years. He's told me about it."

True. But it wasn't like Connor had kept an eye on him all the time. And all of Jared's arrests had been for relatively minor offenses. He wasn't likely to have gotten mixed up with someone truly dangerous.

"Okay, are you sure there's nothing going on in *your* life that could lead to trouble? Any problems follow you here from Las Vegas?" He'd tried asking her questions earlier and she'd gotten pretty defensive. This seemed like a good time to try again. He glanced over at her as they waited at a stoplight. "Did you have any arguments with your brothers-in-law over the value of the business interest you sold them?"

"No. They were fine with it."

Maybe, maybe not. The problem with his line of work was that you couldn't always count on people telling you the truth. Not the whole truth, anyway. Sometimes they were in denial about things. Sometimes they were embarrassed. Sometimes they were hiding something.

"So you leave Las Vegas and come back here to buy the furniture company," he continued as the light changed and they moved forward. "Any problems with that?"

"No."

"Anybody else try to buy it?"

"There was another offer—somebody who wanted to tear the place down and sell off the pieces. There was nothing especially valuable about the land or other assets."

He drove along the perimeter of the lake, trying to keep an eye out for being tailed.

"Do you have any theories at all on what's going on?" he asked after a bit.

"No."

They reached Granite Bay and Connor made the turn, taking a look at the rearview mirror to see if anyone turned with them. It didn't look as if anyone did.

Following Naomi's directions, he continued along the looping road, seeing a few stately houses while others were sheltered behind walls or thick stands of trees.

Finally, she directed him to pull into a driveway in front of a cozy-looking house on the edge of Wolf Lake.

"Thank you for the ride," Naomi said as he came to a stop. "You'll let me know if you hear anything about Jared?"

"Of course." He cut the engine. "But before I go, I want to take a look around. Make sure it's safe."

She looked at him, an expression on her face he couldn't quite figure out.

"It'll just take a few minutes," he added. "And then I'll go."

"Of course," she quickly responded. She glanced out the window, where icy rain was still falling. "It's cold and I know I won't be falling asleep for a while so I'm going to make some coffee. Would you like some? I'm sure I could find us something to eat, too."

"Thanks, but I need to get back into town to talk to some more people before everyone starts heading home for the night." And frankly, he needed a little distance from her to clear his head.

They got out and walked up to the front door, which she unlocked.

"Let me go in first," Connor said, carefully brushing past her.

The fact that the gunmen had seemed like paid hit men weighed on his mind. Professionals typically had backup plans as well as clear motivation to keep trying. They would come after Jared again. Or Naomi. Or both.

Table lights glowed in the front room. "You left these on?"

"They're on timers," she said.

He walked through to the kitchen. A breakfast nook with a bay window afforded a view of the lake. Exterior lights burned on the side of a boathouse at the end of a private pier. "Beautiful view."

Naomi followed him, dropping her phone and purse on the countertop. She pulled a coffee maker toward the edge of the counter and then flicked the lid off a ceramic canister. "I start and end my days right here so I can enjoy the view as much as possible."

She began filling the coffee maker reservoir with water.

"I'm going to check the rest of the first floor and then I'll look upstairs," Connor said.

"Okay. Thank you."

The first floor was sparsely furnished and had the look of a home recently moved into. Connor made quick work of checking it out.

He was halfway to the second floor when he heard the loud *bang* of an explosion from the kitchen, immediately followed by a ribbon of dark smoke.

"Naomi!" He sprinted down the stairs, charging toward the spot where he'd last seen her.

"Naomi!" he called out again.

She didn't answer.

FOUR

She felt the explosion as much as she heard it —the sharp wall of pressure brutally forcing its way across the room.

Afterward, crouched down in front of the heavy steel refrigerator door, which had probably saved her life, Naomi blinked uncomprehendingly for several seconds while trying to figure out what had just happened.

"Naomi!" Connor's voice, breaking through the muffled, cottony sensation in her ears, helped clear her thoughts.

"Here!" she tried to call out, but the wind had been knocked out of her and she barely heard the utterance, herself. Her lungs were tight and her breaths were shallow and it felt like the room had begun to tilt and spin a little.

"Naomi!"

Hearing Connor's voice a second time

strengthened her further and she was finally able to draw in a deeper breath. "Here!" she called out for a second time, much louder than before. "I'm in the kitchen. I'm okay."

At least she thought she was okay. At the moment she wasn't sure of anything.

She'd been leaning inside the refrigerator looking for half-and-half for her coffee when the blast went off. The lights in the kitchen, including inside the fridge, had blinked. She was aware of some kind of fine dust settling on her skin. Plaster, maybe? And dark smoke full of glowing embers making it hard to breathe. Various kitchen items were still making rattling or breaking sounds after being tossed from their normal places by the blast.

In the light made dim by the smoke, she heard and then felt Connor's presence more clearly than she saw him.

"Are you hurt?"

She'd already tried moving her hands and feet. "Everything seems to be in working order. I'm fine." Except for the soreness across her shoulders and the back of her head. "I got walloped pretty good by the fridge door. But it doesn't feel like anything's broken."

"Can you stand?"

"Yeah."

"Here, let me help you."

She took his hand as he quickly helped her to her feet. Her heart nearly stopped when she saw the flames flickering inside the house and beginning to climb up the walls near where the bay window used to be.

"Fire!" she cried out in horror. "My house is on fire!" She turned and frantically looked around. "Where's my phone?"

Connor tapped the screen of his phone and then shoved it at her. "Here." He dashed over to turn on the kitchen faucet full force and then started flinging open cabinet doors as if searching for a container for the water.

"There's a fire extinguisher under the sink," Naomi yelled just before her 9-1-1 call connected.

Connor pulled open the cabinet door and grabbed the extinguisher.

"Nine-one-one, what's your emergency?"

For a few horrifying seconds, Naomi couldn't form the words she wanted to say. So much had happened. So much was happening right now.

She finally managed to explain the situation to the operator while watching Connor squeeze the trigger on the extinguisher, blasting its foamy contents on the flames. The emergency dispatcher confirmed that firefighters were being dispatched to her address before Naomi ended the call.

Wind blew in a steady stream of slushy rain through the blasted-out window, ultimately helping Connor put out the fire.

Naomi's heart continued to pound with fear and adrenaline even after the flames were extinguished. She had come so close to getting killed. The realization of that was terrifying. "I was sitting right there just a couple minutes ago," she said hoarsely. The wind blowing into the house had cleared out much of the smoke, but her throat and eyes still felt scratchy. "I sit by that window all the time. I would have sat there tonight as soon as my coffee was ready."

"The placement of the explosive wasn't a random choice." Connor split his attention between the destroyed bay window and the passages from the connecting living room on one end and dining room on the other, making certain no one could sneak up on them from inside the house. He drew a gun from the holster under his jacket and kept it pointed toward the ground. Until that moment it hadn't occurred to Naomi that whoever had caused the explosion might be inside her house.

"You think the killers have been watching me for a while?"

Connor sighed heavily. "Looks that way. They knew exactly where to place the explosive."

Naomi looked down and spotted a bent and blackened metal cylinder on the floor. A pipe bomb. Thrown through the window. Beside it were the splintered and partly charred table and the chair where she normally sat, tumbled over and blown apart so that they looked more like a pile of wood than furniture.

Dear Lord, thank You for Your protection.

"I'm going to make sure the flames weren't able to take hold on the outside of the house," Connor said. "And that there isn't anyone out there, watching and waiting to attack again after we think the danger is over."

Goose bumps rippled over the surface of Naomi's skin. She kept a close eye on him as he carefully opened the side door a few paces away from the destroyed bay window and cautiously stepped outside.

He had his gun in his hand, and Naomi couldn't help imagining the bomber waiting outside, also with a gun. She moved as close to the open doorway as she dared, hoping that the darkness would keep Connor hidden from any potential assailants. And that she would be out of view of any potential assailants, too.

Icy rainwater blowing through the open door

fanned across her and she only now began to feel cold. Maybe the sudden jolt of adrenaline after the explosion had started to ease off. "Do you see anything?" she called out, suddenly afraid that Connor had been attacked without her knowing it.

Several slow-moving seconds later, she heard footsteps and then he came back inside. He was completely soaked. "I didn't see any flames. Looks like the rain kept the fire from taking hold and spreading. And I didn't see anyone out there. Although it would be easy enough for them to hide in the darkness."

Approaching sirens wailed outside.

"The police will be arriving with the fire department," Naomi said wearily. "At least that should scare the bad guys away."

"For now," Connor said.

Naomi's shoulders slumped. "You think they'll come back."

"I'd say it's undeniable that somebody *really* wants you dead. So, probably. Yes. I think they'll try again."

Raindrops spattered against the black plastic garbage bags that Connor had taped over the blown-out bay window to help protect the interior of Naomi's house from the elements. It was a short-term fix until he could get something better in place. And he was already working on taking care of that.

"You're certain you can't think of anyone who would be targeting you?" Detective Romanov stood on the other side of the kitchen island and directed her question at Naomi.

"I'm sure. It's my brother who's crossed paths with criminals." She shook her head. "Somehow it's got to be connected to him. Maybe the actual drug dealers he was arrested with don't want him to testify against them."

Connor knew that Jared did plan to testify in return for reduced or possibly dropped charges. Jared had told him. But even if they were convicted, the actual jail time the dealers would face would be fairly low. It didn't make sense that they'd risk adding murder to the other charges against them.

The detective gave Naomi an appraising look, glanced at Connor and then turned back to her. "Let's talk in private."

"No." Naomi stepped slightly closer to Connor. "I can say whatever I need to right here."

Maybe he was kidding himself, but it felt to Connor as if that declaration *meant* something. Like maybe despite everything she still trusted him enough to rely on him.

Or maybe she was just rattled after a rough evening, and her decision had nothing to do with him personally at all.

He took a deep breath, trying to push aside the memories of their last big fight twenty years ago, as he gazed around the kitchen.

Emergency responders had arrived quickly, with the fire department confirming that there were no lingering, hidden flames outside. They'd left the incendiary device untouched on the floor for the cops to process for fingerprints or any other evidence they could find. Detective Romanov had arrived close behind the patrol officers.

After bagging the pipe bomb and then closely examining the damaged window, inside and out, she'd instructed the sergeant who'd arrived with her to take pictures and then given Connor the go-ahead to do what he could to limit the amount of rainwater soaking Naomi's wall and floor. At that point he'd sent a text to his business manager and longtime friend, Maribel Fast Horse, asking her to have someone come out with plywood so he could put up a more substantial—and secure—covering in place of the plastic bags.

Romanov had offered to interview Naomi in the living room where it was warmer and brighter, but Naomi had wanted to stay in the kitchen and nook area where she could clean a little as she talked. Connor remembered that tendency back when they were together. When she was tense or nervous she liked to *do* things. And if he tried to help she saw it as him getting in her way. He'd learned to be careful about that.

"I saw security cameras on the exterior of your house," the detective said. "I'll need you to send me your security footage for this evening."

"Actually, I don't have any." Naomi glanced at Connor before turning back to the detective. "I've been so busy with moving here and taking over the furniture company I just bought that I haven't had time to contact a security company and get everything up and running. The previous owners left those cameras behind but they don't connect to anything."

She'd always known Range River to be a relatively safe town so she hadn't been in a hurry to get it done.

The side door opened and a police sergeant along with a detective walked in, slushy rain covering their hats and jackets. "The weather hid any tracks," the detective said. "We did a full walkaround on the property and couldn't find anything."

"Talk to the neighbors and ask if they've got security video. I realize it's getting late but I'm sure the sirens already woke everybody up." Romanov pressed her lips tightly together for a moment. "We need to get a lead on this, quickly. It has the feel of something bigger than a personal grudge."

The two cops headed back outside.

Connor's phone chimed. At the same time, the detective got a notification, as well.

Connor looked at his screen. "Maribel and Hugh are here."

Romanov nodded. "I'll tell my officers to let them in."

Moments later a charcoal-haired woman in her mid-fifties and a tall man of roughly the same age with curly brown hair came through the house and into the kitchen. The man carried a sheet of plywood. A uniformed officer, also carrying plywood, followed them in. The woman gripped the handle of a toolbox in one hand and a power drill in the other.

They set their items down while offering a general greeting to everyone in the room.

Naomi turned to Connor with slightly lifted eyebrows.

Of course she was curious. She didn't know who they were. Connor and Maribel had worked together for so long that it was hard to believe she and Naomi had never met. Hugh was a friend Maribel had met at church quite a while ago, but she'd recently started spending time with him apart from church services, which was both a delight and worry for her adult son, Wade.

Connor made the introductions, and when he said Naomi's name he saw Maribel's eyes widen slightly.

Shortly after Connor and Naomi parted ways, Connor's father and stepmother were killed in an auto accident and Connor took on the raising of his two younger half-siblings, Danny and Hayley, who had been only eleven and seven years old at the time. Connor had been twenty-one, and while he hadn't felt prepared to be a single parent, he'd seen no other option. Danny had a best buddy named Wade. And Wade's mom, Maribel, at roughly a decade older than Connor and with much more experience at child-rearing, had been an immeasurable help to Connor.

The early years were tough, financially and emotionally, but Connor and Maribel lived near each other and helped one another out. Connor took a job as a bounty hunter and eventually formed his own company, Range River

Bail Bonds. He quickly hired Maribel, and they'd been business partners ever since.

Maribel had also been the one person he'd talked to—just a little—about Naomi back when he was still trying to process what had happened and what he'd done wrong. He'd also been trying to decide whether he should take another try at marriage or accept that he was not good husband material.

Over the years, by default, he'd chosen to stay single. He'd dated a little, but he'd never felt sure that he could make the women happy long-term after the failure of his first marriage, so none of the relationships had lasted. Eventually he just stopped dating.

His brother and sister were aware that he had been married once, a long time ago. But it wasn't something he ever talked about with them. It now occurred to Connor that they probably didn't even know her name.

Hugh and the officer helping him had already moved to the bay window, where they set down the plywood and began to pull down the plastic bags.

"Maribel, I'm almost ready for the drill."

Hugh's voice appeared to snap Maribel out of her fascination with Naomi. She schooled her features, offered her a smile and a nod, and started walking toward Hugh. But not without shooting Connor a meaningful glance.

"I have something to show you," Detective Romanov said to Naomi after taking a moment to tap the screen of her tablet. "I had some mug shots put together based on the descriptions that you gave us earlier. I'd intended to call you down to the station in the morning to look at them. But since we're all here, how about you take a look now?"

The power drill made intermittent shrieking sounds while Hugh secured the boards in place as the detective set her tablet on the kitchen island and slid it over so that both Connor and Naomi could look at it.

"Have you heard anything from your brother?" the detective asked quietly.

Blinking rapidly, Naomi wiped away the tears that quickly formed and fell down her cheeks. "No, I haven't. I've tried to call several times, but he doesn't answer, and he hasn't called me back."

Beside her, Connor resisted the urge to do something comforting in the moment. Like wrap his arms around her. Maybe give her a kiss on the top of her head.

Whoa. Where did that come from?

Immediately realizing the absurdity of his

thoughts, he crossed his arms over his chest. They had happened to cross paths because of his business relationship with her brother. There was nothing personal about it *at all*. If he was reading anything more into her behavior around him he was just fooling himself. Any relationship between the two of them was completely in the past. He needed to remember that.

Naomi began swiping the mug shots on the tablet. Connor looked down at them, as well. He recognized many of the photos as either pictures he'd seen before or as individuals he'd actually come in contact with, usually through his work. The familiar ones he recognized as men who'd been accused and sometimes convicted of assault, extortion, strong-arm robbery and other violent crimes comparable to what Naomi had faced today.

Naomi kept swiping until she came to a familiar image. "The black-haired man," she said, her voice shaky. "He shot at me at the very beginning. Told me I'd taken long enough to get there. Like he'd been waiting for me."

Romanov glanced down at the photo and nodded. "His name is Sergio Almada."

"What do you know about him?" Connor asked.

The detective nodded down at the tablet.

"Keep going. I'm certain you're going to see his accomplice very soon."

After a few more swipes, Naomi came to the second man, with the long brown hair. "This man," she said before looking up at Romanov.

"Okay." She reached for the tablet. "That would be Ladd Olsen. I expected as much. The two of them often work together and they *are* professionals." She directed her comments to Connor. "Just as you suspected."

"Professional what?" Naomi asked. *"Killers?"*

"Both have been charged with assault and strong-arm robbery. The suspicion is that they've done a lot more that they have not yet been charged with. The last time they were arrested, they made bail and then went underground. Homicide detectives out of Las Vegas have been looking for them not only because they jumped bail but also to potentially face new charges that I can't talk about. Almada lived here in Range River for a while about ten years ago. He still has friends in the area. That's why Las Vegas Homicide contacted us and forwarded their photos several months ago. I suspect they came out this way to lie low— and that while they're here, they've started working for someone locally."

"Like the Invaders, maybe?" Connor asked. "It sounds like the crimes these two commit are right up their alley." Leaders of the Invaders outlaw motorcycle gang earned money through various illegal enterprises and in a few short years had gained power and influence in the local criminal underground.

"Stay away from the gang," Romanov said sternly. "Almada and Olsen are bail jumpers, so as a bounty hunter you can legitimately go after them. But don't go sniffing around the Invaders. You've got no jurisdiction there."

Connor nodded. "Understood." Local, state and possibly federal law enforcement had joined in to take down the gang and Connor had been warned on previous manhunts to keep himself and everyone in his employ away from them. "Naomi recently moved here from Las Vegas," he added, thinking out loud. "The Las Vegas connection could be something meaningful. Or it could just be a coincidence."

The detective tilted her head slightly. "Do you know each other personally, beyond your business transaction with her brother?"

Had he not mentioned that earlier?

"We used to be married," Naomi said. "But that was a long time ago."

Romanov gave Connor a dark look and then arched a slender auburn eyebrow. He was certain that he would need to reassure her later that he hadn't intentionally withheld that information. He didn't want to get on her bad side. Bounty hunters were not law enforcement officers. It was the detective's discretion as to whether she would share information with him on a case or completely ice him out.

After a moment Romanov turned her attention to Naomi. "Tell me a little more about your life in Las Vegas."

Naomi summarized what she'd told Connor while the detective listened without interruption. "What kind of business was it?" she finally asked.

"Outdoor gear. Much of it designed especially for desert climates and terrain."

"And how did your late husband's family feel about your inheritance?"

Naomi seemed at a loss for words for a moment before answering. "No one seemed angry about it." She shook her head. "None of them complained to me about it."

"I see."

The other detective and sergeant returned from canvassing the neighborhood. Nobody had seen or heard anything unusual. The houses on either side of Naomi's house and across the street did have security cameras, but they were too far away to pick up good images of the outside of her house.

"We did get some footage of street traffic from earlier this evening. It's pretty sparse, not a lot of vehicles drove by, but maybe it will end up helping."

"Okay," the detective said. "Let's take a look at it when we get back to the station."

At that point the damaged window had been temporarily repaired and the police were wrapping up.

"If I were you, I wouldn't stay here tonight," Romanov said to Naomi.

"You can stay with me," Connor offered.

Naomi cast him a doubtful glance.

"I own the old Riverside Inn. It's my private residence now. My adopted brother Wade and his new wife, Charlotte, live there with me."

"Adopted brother?"

"Wade is Maribel's son. When we have guests, Maribel usually stays there, too, to help take care of things."

Connor was aware that his friend and business partner could hear everything he said. She and Hugh had remained after finishing the repairs in case Connor needed any further help from them. He glanced over and she smiled and nodded at him. "I'd be happy to stay at the inn and help out."

"There's plenty of room," Connor continued. "You'll be safer with us than you would be if you checked into a hotel."

"You should take him up on that offer," Romanov said to Naomi. "I don't know how long it will take us to figure out what's going on and put a stop to it. We're doing everything we can. But we can't be everywhere all the time. You'd be wise to allow Connor and his family to keep you safe."

Tension grabbed tight hold of Connor as he worried that Naomi would turn down his offer. He was afraid of what might happen to her if she did.

After another moment's hesitation, and a glance toward the boarded-up bay window, Naomi finally said, "Okay."

Connor didn't feel the wave of relief he'd anticipated. Instead, his mind was racing, imagining how someone might try to get at her the next time. Because it was obvious there *would be* a next time, and he had no way to anticipate what form the next deadly attack would take.

FIVE

Riding beside Connor in his truck brought back memories for Naomi.

She kept glancing at him, grateful that his focus on the road and their surroundings meant he probably hadn't noticed that she couldn't seem to keep her eyes off him.

Maribel and Hugh were in an SUV behind them for extra protection as they headed for the Riverside Inn.

Naomi's thoughts had been in turmoil all through the long, terrible afternoon and evening. From her brother's initial phone call all the way to the explosion in her house, it felt like she hadn't had five minutes to really sit and process.

It was only now, after leaving her house and sliding into the warmth of Connor's truck cab, that she'd been able to slow the inner whirlwind of emotions enough to focus on her feelings about seeing him again.

They'd been deeply and irrevocably in love—or so they'd thought—as teenagers believing nothing could ever break them apart. They'd thought they knew everything at the time and that they were so grown-up, so ready to face the future together. She laughed softly.

"What?" Connor asked.

She shook her head, unable to suppress the faint smile still on her lips. "Nothing. Just nerves, probably."

They were certain they had life all figured out when they'd gotten married. After all, they loved each other, and what on earth could matter more than that? How her heart used to race whenever she was near him. He'd made her so happy. She'd thought their life together would be filled with nothing but joy.

And then they'd faced heartbreak and sorrow like neither of them had ever known before— along with the unanswerable question of why their unborn child would be taken from them before he could even draw his first breath. Neither of them had been a person of faith at the time. Neither had been offered much in the way of support from their parents. They had

nothing and no one to lean on but each other...
and that hadn't been enough.

Connor had always struggled to express
himself, especially when it came to his emotions, but at that time, he shut down completely. The man she loved seemed to have
vanished, leaving an ice-cold stranger in his
place. In the end, Naomi had decided that she
couldn't stay with someone who could shut her
out like that. In hindsight, she knew that she
should have been more patient, should have
tried harder to reach him, but at the time, she
had felt like she was drowning—it had been
all she could do to keep her head above water.
She hadn't had the strength to throw anyone
else a lifeline.

And so they'd gone their separate ways, and
that was that.

She was alarmed to realize she was feeling
a stirring of emotion for him as she sat beside
him right now. A rippling delight of sorts, despite the awful situation they were in. It was
subtle, but she recognized it as a stirring of
the old love she used to feel for him. And she
was immediately determined to tamp it down.
She was just tired and scared and searching
for comfort. And Connor happened to be right
beside her.

They were not a good match. She knew that for a fact. People didn't change.

Ah, but they do change. You did.

Maturity. Life experience. The grace of God. Those elements did change people.

More disquieting thoughts along those lines brought with them a boatload of confusion and uncertainty. What did she think? What did she know? What did she *want*, now that she'd been a widow for two years? Would she like to ever be married again? Up until a moment ago, that question had been the furthest thing from her mind. But now...

"Here it is, home sweet home." Connor turned into a driveway that curved through an expanse of tall, thick pine trees and then opened onto a small parking lot with a full view of a beautifully rustic two-story building. Though it had originally been built in the 1880s, it had clearly been brought up to modern standards while still maintaining its Old West charm.

There was a flash of lights in her side mirror as Maribel and Hugh had turned into the parking lot behind them.

"The Riverside Inn," Naomi said. "The last time I saw this place the property was overrun with pine saplings and wild blackberry vines." Hiking to the romantically overgrown inn, with its grounds leading all the way down to the edge of the deep, swift Range River, had been a common adventure for local teens.

Icy rain continued to fall steadily, but between the passes of the windshield wipers she could see the gorgeous river-stone exterior and the thick wooden beams that had managed to survive nearly a hundred and fifty years.

"The foundation stayed sound despite the neglect," Connor said. "It makes for a strong, solid home where you'll be protected. We've got excellent security." He glanced out his side window. "Including cameras and lights and motion sensors in the parking lot and the surrounding trees so no one can sneak up on us."

Naomi gave him a sharp look. "Do you have a lot of people coming out here to try to attack you?"

He shook his head. "The Range River Bail Bonds offices are in town. Most attacks against us are focused there. We don't bring clients out here. And thanks to the video cameras, we've been able to stop the handful of attempts at break-ins or attacks before they started. Given what we do for a living, and the people we interact with, we do need to be careful. Beyond that, it makes a good refuge for me and my family when we just need that feeling of to-getherness. And it's a good place to bring peo-ple, like you, when they're in danger."

They got out of the truck and he grabbed the suitcases Naomi had packed before they left her house.

"Why do you want to help dangerous peo-ple?" Naomi asked as they walked toward the massive front door. Maribel and Hugh were already in front of them. "Why bail criminals out of jail? How did you even get started doing that?"

"People are presumed innocent until proven guilty," he said. "Our justice system is based on that assumption. It has to be, because the truth is that sometimes an innocent person is charged with a crime they didn't commit. If a judge sets bail, the accused is entitled to pur-chase a bond and go free until their next court date or until a trial is held to resolve the issue.

"As far as your question of how I got started, after my dad and stepmom died, someone had to take care of Danny and Hayley, so I stepped up to do it."

Of course you did. Naomi wasn't surprised. It sounded like something Connor would do.

"I was desperate for a job that would pay enough so I could support them. I met a bounty hunter who liked his job, thought I'd be suited for it and suggested I give it a try, so I did. Things went well. The job offered the opportunity to earn more money if I worked harder and I liked that. The hours were flexible, which made it easier to deal with the kids and school and babysitter schedules and all that kind of stuff. The job put my safety at risk, which wasn't ideal when raising children, but at the time I didn't have any other job skills that could bring enough income to support all of us."

"That sounds overwhelming," Naomi said as they stepped up to the covered porch, where Maribel and Hugh were waiting. As soon as they arrived, Hugh said good-night, with an especially warm smile directed at Maribel, and then left.

Connor glanced at Maribel. "Life was exhausting when Danny and Wade and Hayley were little. Maribel and I took turns looking after the kids. There were days when I didn't think I was going to make it."

Maribel laughed. "Me, too."

"Now all three of them are grown and married," he said. "I look at them and wonder where the time has gone."

Naomi couldn't be certain, but she thought

she heard a catch in his voice as he turned and tapped a code into a security keypad before pulling on the door after it unlatched.

"Prepare yourself to be exuberantly greeted," he said just as Naomi heard the riotous sounds of dogs barking and multiple paws tapping toward them on a wooden floor. "I have dogs," he said, "and they love people."

"So they're not watchdogs?"

"Well, they're certainly not likely to attack intruders, but don't worry, they'll let us know if anyone comes creeping around."

While the historic inn had been vacant back when Naomi was a small child, it had been locked and boarded up too carefully for anyone to be able to sneak in and look around, so she'd never seen the interior before. She stepped inside to a foyer and beyond it a great room with an oversize fireplace made of smooth river stones and floor-to-ceiling windows, which she figured must offer stunning views of the Range River during daylight hours. The high ceiling, supported by thick wooden beams, soared up above the second floor. There was an upstairs gallery, where Naomi could see doors that she assumed led to bedrooms.

"It's gorgeous." She reached down to pet a tiny wire-haired dog with a noticeable underbite who was standing on her foot. "Hello." The three other dogs, prancing with excitement, moved closer toward her.

"That's Joey," Connor said, indicating the dog on her foot as he set Naomi's suitcases onto the hardwood floor. He then went on to introduce her to the other dogs, along with a couple of cats that came halfway down the staircase to have a look at her. Two more were in front of the fire in the fireplace, and both gave her a mild look before curling back up again. Connor told her their names, as well.

A man and woman, probably in their thirties, walked out from the kitchen. The man looked like Maribel. The woman, blue-eyed with light blond hair, looked familiar, though Naomi couldn't place her.

"This is my son, Wade," Maribel said. "And his wife, Charlotte."

Charlotte.

"Charlotte Halstead?" Naomi asked. The Halstead family owned the luxury resort on the edge of Wolf Lake. Pictures of the twin daughters, Charlotte and Dinah, had figured prominently in resort advertising from the time the girls were small. As a result, they were well-known in Range River.

"That would be me," Charlotte said with a

smile. "Pleased to meet you." Her smile softened. "I'm sorry it's under such terrible circumstances. But I want you to know that the Range River bounty hunters do very good work. My sister got into some trouble that ended up putting me in danger." She glanced at her husband. "That's how I met Wade. He and the whole team did a lot to help."

"We'll do everything we can to find your brother," Wade added.

"I appreciate that."

It was encouraging to know that there were so many people looking for her brother. It gave her hope that the good guys would find him before those thugs from earlier could strike again. But Naomi couldn't help thinking of how quickly things had gone from normal to deadly, or potentially deadly, today. In an instant, Kevin Ashton's life had ended. If she hadn't been standing at the refrigerator when the explosion went off in her breakfast nook, she might be dead right now, as well. She had no idea where Jared was and it seemed likely Kevin's killers would be looking for him, too. Naomi still didn't know why they'd been targeted in the first place, but now that both she and Jared had witnessed the men committing murder, they had very strong motives to want them both silenced for good.

"I know you must be exhausted," Maribel said to Naomi. "And probably hungry. Come with me and I'll get you something to eat."

"Thank you, but I'm not really hungry."

"Well at least let me get you something to drink. A glass of cool water, if nothing else. I know you've been through a lot and you're worried about your brother, but you need to take care of yourself."

"She makes a good point," Connor said softly.

Connor hadn't mentioned in any of his introductions that Naomi was his former wife. She didn't quite know what to think about that. Was it a topic she needed to avoid when talking to his family and friends? Had he never told them about her? Did he want to keep their failed marriage a secret?

She agreed to go with Maribel into the kitchen and the others followed. Some kind of conversation was inevitable, and she made up her mind to say whatever seemed appropriate in the moment and not worry about explaining about her former place in Connor's life.

The kitchen was spacious and had a wooden dining table where Connor pulled out a chair for Naomi. She sank into it, and before she knew it there was a glass of water by her elbow. She sipped it as Connor sat next to her.

She took a deep breath and blew it out. For a moment or two she felt herself on the edge of being able to relax. But the images of the events she'd witnessed during the day popped back into her mind, tightening her stomach, making her heart race as she felt thrown back into the horrifying experiences. It was the oddest sensation of being here at the kitchen table and back in the moment of seeing Kevin's lifeless body, or being shot at, or dropping down to her knees at the sound of an explosion all at the same time.

She started to feel light-headed.

"Breathe," Connor said beside her.

She forced in a deep breath, and then another.

Maribel set a small bowl of ice cream in front of her and another in front of Connor. "Maybe you could eat a few bites," she said.

It was a kind gesture and Naomi managed to eat a little. The sugary sweetness *did* seem to help clear her head a little, making it easier to ground herself in the here and now.

Maribel, Wade and Charlotte all came to the table, eating ice cream, and talking quietly without asking anything of Naomi, which was a relief.

The flashbacks had stopped for now, but she still felt overwhelmed by everything she had experienced. She started to tremble. Emotions, like hurling dark waves, built up inside her. She needed to process it all without an audience. Cry, maybe, or perhaps just curl up in a ball and lie on a bed. After that, maybe she could get some sleep. And in the morning, she could get back to looking for her brother.

A short time later, Connor and Maribel walked her upstairs to a bedroom with an en suite bath.

"If you need anything, just ask," Connor said from the doorway after Maribel had walked away.

Naomi nodded. "Thank you."

They exchanged good-nights and she closed the door.

The image of Connor, concern evident in his eyes, stayed in her mind. He had already taken personal risks to help her. And if she knew Connor, he would take more. She was not only worried about her brother, but also about her former husband. If Connor hadn't been targeted already for helping her, he probably would be, soon. And very vicious people would be coming after him as they tried to get to her.

* * *

"This is my sister, Hayley, and her husband, Jack." Connor stood in his home office at the Riverside Inn the next morning, managing the last of the introductions. He was anxious to give everyone their marching orders so they could get busy looking for Jared and the two murderous bail jumpers he desperately wanted to bring to justice.

"Pleased to meet you," Hayley and Jack each said to Naomi.

Naomi stared at Hayley for a moment, before finally shaking her head slightly and then smiling. "The last time I met you, you were just a tiny little thing. I think you were about five or six years old."

Hayley had just turned twenty-seven.

"Oh, have we met before?" Hayley said, turning to Connor with an unconvincing expression of confusion on her face.

Connor had no doubt his sister knew that Naomi was his former wife. He glanced at Maribel, who gave him a guilty half smile before looking away. Of course Maribel would have overheard Connor and Naomi telling Detective Romanov about their history in Naomi's kitchen last night. That conversation would have confirmed that this was Connor's ex-wife, and she would have told his siblings. Connor didn't blame her and he wasn't angry about it.

"Naomi and I were married for a short while," he said, to clear the air. "It was a long time ago."

"I see," Hayley said quietly and Connor silently dared her to ask for any further details. She must have picked up on his mood because she didn't ask for a further explanation. Instead, she took a moment to explain to Naomi that her husband was also a bounty hunter and that he owned a bail bonds business of his own.

"So I'm assuming you're Danny," Naomi said, turning to Connor's brother. "You would have been about ten when I last saw you."

"Yes, ma'am." Of course Danny had taken off his cowboy hat when he'd walked into the inn. He held it in his hand right now, fingering the brim as though he were nervous.

"I don't suppose you remember me?" Naomi said.

Danny cast a glance at Connor before turning back to her. "Actually, I didn't until now. But after seeing you… I believe I do remember you. Did Connor used to like to ride his bike with you sitting on the handlebars?"

"Yes!" Naomi laughed and for a moment it

appeared to Connor that the haunted and fearful expression he'd seen in her eyes from the moment he caught up with her at the sawmill lifted, at least for a little while. "We crashed a few times with me sitting there, too."

Slowly, her smile faded. And the aggravating ache in Connor's heart that she seemed to draw out grew stronger.

"Everybody sit down and let's get to work," he said in his sharpest "boss man" voice before clearing his throat. None of them needed a stroll down memory lane. His crew just needed to do what they always did: hunt down and capture bad guys. The morning would get away from them if they didn't hurry up and get moving.

His office had a large desk in one corner but otherwise looked more like a den. While the others sat on thickly upholstered sofas, he moved to his desk chair, where he had to pick up a snoozing cat before he could sit down.

"I assume everyone's read the notes I texted you earlier this morning," Connor started.

Maribel and the bounty hunters nodded. While Maribel rarely went out on physical pursuits, she was invaluable at online research and team coordination.

"Good. I want all four of you working together to find Sergio Almada and Ladd Olsen. I'm going with the working assumption that they're sticking together. We know how dangerous they are and I want all of you working together so you can watch each other's backs. Start with your confidential informants. I've never come across these two before but apparently they're fairly big players in Las Vegas with ties to the local underworld here in Range River. That suggests to me that they're smart, they're good at hiding their tracks and that someone locally is helping them out. They've probably been here a few months—long enough that someone should know *something* about them. We just need to find that someone."

"What about Jared?" Naomi asked. "Isn't finding him our priority?"

"It is. You and I are going to look for him. Given the assumption that our two hired gunmen are trying to track him down, too, having my team searching for those two means that if they get on the trail of Almada and Olsen they'll possibly be on the trail of your brother, as well. At the very least, if they can take those two off the streets, you and your brother should be safer."

Should be safer. Connor had chosen his

words carefully because he still had no idea what Jared had gotten into. Or who was after him and Naomi. Somebody was paying Almada and Olsen, and he still had no idea who.

"Do you want us to start by going to Jared's apartment?" Naomi asked. "He gave me a key for emergencies when I first moved back."

Connor shook his head. "That's not the first place I want to go. The cops must have gone there last night to look for him, but I'm pretty sure he would have avoided the place for exactly that reason. Eventually I want to go talk with his neighbors, but not just yet."

"Won't the police have already tried that?" she asked.

"Probably, but we want to find anybody who knows something who won't talk to cops but *will* talk to us. Some people don't trust police but they do want to keep trouble out of their own neighborhoods."

"So where are we going to start?" she asked.

"First off, you don't have to go anywhere if you don't want to go. You would be safer staying at the inn. Honestly, that's what I'd prefer that you do."

Even as he made the offer, he knew that she wouldn't take him up on it. As expected, she shook her head. "If things get bad, I will happily hide out here. But first, I want to go with you. I still believe what I told you earlier, that Jared is more likely to give himself up if he sees me out looking for him. That's what I'm hoping will happen. Or that he'll hear from someone that I'm out trying to find him and then he'll contact me so I can talk him into turning himself in."

"Okay." Connor took a breath. He didn't think she was going to like what he said next. "Our first stop will be your dad's house."

He was pretty sure she blanched a little.

"Why?" She made a scoffing sound. "Do you really think my dad would help Jared? Give him a place to hide? Especially when doing that could put Dad in danger?" She shook her head. "Please."

"Maybe he'll give us some useful information. It's worth a try."

Her response confirmed what he'd already guessed. That she and her dad were still not on good terms. They hadn't been all those years ago when she was a teen and her dad was a violent alcoholic.

"All right." Naomi drew herself up. She lifted her chin, her worried expression turning defiant. "I'll talk to him. I'll do whatever it takes to find Jared."

Her voice broke when she said her brother's name. Connor's own heart broke a little seeing her like that.

"How recently have you seen your dad?"

"It's been years," she said flatly, wiping her eyes.

"Well, from what I've seen and heard from Jared, he hasn't changed much. Which means he still hangs around other criminals." *Other* criminals, because Greg Santelli was himself a thief and a brawler, an occasional drug dealer and a man who'd done time over the years for strong-arm robbery and blackmail. "I'm afraid some of his cronies wouldn't think twice about carrying out a contract hit on you or Jared if the price was right."

"I'm not sure my dad wouldn't do it *himself* if the price was right."

Connor wished he could tell her she was exaggerating, but he didn't think she was. "When we get to your dad's property, make sure you stay close to me. Keep an eye on our surroundings while we're there. And if he wants to speak to you alone, don't agree to it."

"I understand."

He glanced around the room at his team. "All right, let's get to work."

He hadn't heard anything from Detective

Romanov yet this morning, which meant that she and her crew hadn't found Jared and cracked the case overnight.

The last thing he wanted was for this case to drag on. If the bad guys decided to lie low for a while and the cops turned their attention to other, newer, cases, Naomi would be all the more vulnerable when the thugs decided to attack her again. Plus, there was no telling what might happen to Jared.

Connor glanced at his phone for a quick look at the video footage from all the cameras placed around the property, just to make sure Naomi would be safe when they stepped outside.

Beyond that, as they moved through town, he couldn't be certain of her safety at all. He would have to assume the whole time that she was a clearly marked target and someone was watching and ready to take a shot at her at any moment.

SIX

Her dad's house was back in the woods, of course.

"Away from prying eyes," Naomi said to Connor. "The way he prefers it whenever possible." Using the term *dad* for Greg Santelli always stuck in her throat a little. She couldn't remember precisely when she'd realized from movies and TV shows what dads were supposed to be like. She'd probably been around nine or ten. The man who'd fathered her was nothing like the caring family figures in her favorite programs. "When we lived in town, he was always paranoid about Jared and I leaving the garage door open, because he had stolen stuff in there that he planned to sell." She shook her head. "Some of the items were things he'd stolen from our own neighbors."

"You still sure you want to do this?" Connor asked as they drove up to the dilapidated single-story house with several equally shoddy storage buildings near it.

A haphazard barbed wire fence had been rolled around the cluster of buildings. Clearly it was not there to keep animals in, but to make it harder for a random thief to drive up and help themselves to whatever wasn't nailed down. Dear old Dad was trying to protect his property from people just like himself.

Naomi nodded. "I'll do whatever it takes to find Jared."

She started feeling jittery as they passed through an open gate and drove up to the house. Suddenly thirsty, she tried to moisten her lips and ignore the feeling of her dry tongue sticking to the roof of her mouth. She had no reason to fear Greg Santelli. He had no power over her anymore, and if he tried to threaten or attack her, she knew that Connor would intervene. The years when she'd had a reason to hide from her dad were way in the past.

Still, the memories remained. Memories of him and her mom both fighting and screaming at each other. Strange, drunken behavior that was terrifying to a child. People coming and going at odd hours. The fairly frequent backhanded slaps for no apparent reason. And then there were the strangers coming and going at odd hours. Buying drugs, she reasoned now. Or coming to the house for some other nefarious reason. Sometimes, she wondered how she'd survived her childhood. Frankly, it was shocking that her father was still alive—her mother had passed ten years ago.

She glanced at Connor, grateful for his presence. He'd made her feel safer back in the day. He made her feel safer now.

She glanced out the window at the grass, looking yellowed and scrubby since the weather had turned biting cold. Of course there were evergreen trees nearby. This was North Idaho. But she couldn't help settling her gaze on the broad-leaved trees, the birches and elms, with their missing or darkened leaves barely still hanging on this late in the year.

Her brother had been fifteen and Naomi had just turned eighteen when she'd found out she was pregnant and married Connor, finally getting out from under her parents' roof for good. "I shouldn't have left him behind," she muttered, blinking rapidly as her eyes burned and her stomach felt unsettled.

"Jared?" Connor asked, braking to a stop by the front door. "You might have legally been an adult when you moved out, but you were really just a kid yourself at the time. It wasn't your job to parent him."

It was kind of Connor to say, but she knew in her heart that he was wrong. Jared was her little brother. She shouldn't have abandoned him. Especially when she knew what she was leaving him to face.

Too soon, before she'd had time to emotionally steel herself, the front door of the house flew open and a figure stepped out onto the wooden porch.

The slump-shouldered bully loomed so much larger in her memories.

"Have you seen your dad since you moved back to town?" Connor asked.

Naomi shook her head. "I've had no reason to." And certainly no desire to.

She grabbed the door handle, yanked on it and stepped out of the truck. The only way to approach Greg Santelli was to move boldly toward him. Otherwise, he'd read you as weak and start pushing his own agenda. She'd learned that a long time ago.

"Dad."

He shaded his eyes with his hand to get a better look at her. "Naomi?"

"Yes."

It was only three steps up to the porch, but

she didn't climb them. Instead, she stood on the dying early-winter grass, arms crossed over her chest, chin up and shoulders back. No way she would let him know he still managed to trigger fear within her.

"We're looking for Jared," she said, as Connor stepped up beside her.

Greg shifted his eyes toward the bounty hunter before turning his gaze back to his daughter. Considering the life Greg had chosen, and the fact that Jared had needed to be bonded out of jail in the past, she was fairly certain he knew about Connor's profession. In the end, it didn't matter if he did know. She just wanted answers to her questions and then she'd be gone.

Greg blinked, and in an instant he had the old predatory smile on his face.

She turned toward Connor. "He knows I bought the furniture factory," she said quietly. They were far enough away that Greg wouldn't hear her. "He figures I've got money and he's trying to decide how he can manipulate this situation to get some." She needed to say it out loud to remind herself of who Greg was. Because some part of her still wanted to believe, despite everything, that he would be unselfishly willing to help her or Jared when they needed him. And that was ridiculous.

"Want me to take over?" Connor asked quietly.

"No, I can handle it."

She watched Connor glance at the nearby tree line with the dark forest beyond, at the storage buildings, and at the old cars and trucks on the property. "Try to handle it quickly, okay? Your father might not be the only person here. If he's got company, they're probably not the kind of people we want to linger around any longer than we absolutely have to."

"Right." She glanced at the covered windows of the house. A frisson of nerves moved up her spine, leaving the hairs on the nape of her neck on end. No telling what went on in there. And now, whether it was rational or not, she had the feeling she was being watched.

"Jared," she prompted her father, who still had not come down the three steps to greet her. No surprise there. "Have you seen him or heard from him since late yesterday afternoon?"

"I have not. And you know, I'm worried about that boy. I heard what happened to you and him last night and I was sorry to hear about it."

A curtain moved at one of the front windows.

"You have company?" Connor asked.

"My son's not here," Greg said, deflecting

the question. "He's got his own place in town. You know that. I'd rather see him caught by you than killed by whoever came after him. I'll ask around. See what I can learn."

The curtain moved again.

"Let's get out of here," Connor said softly.

"Thanks for your help," Naomi said, doing her best to hide her sarcasm.

"I'd like to see you again," Greg said. "Maybe we could talk about old times and what you've got planned now that you're back here in town. But next time, call first."

"Right," she said, exchanging phone numbers with him. For Jared's sake, she needed to make herself available to the man she normally avoided.

They walked back to the truck. Naomi noticed that Connor did not turn his back on Greg or the front of the house on the way there.

"Somebody's in that house," Naomi said as soon as they were in the truck. "Maybe it's my brother. Can't you demand to go in and look around? Don't your bounty hunter *powers* allow you to do that?"

"Powers?" Connor fired up the engine, scanning the area around them, his gaze continually shifting from the house to the outbuildings, to the shadowy tree line and back again. "Jared gave Range River Bail Bonds the right to search his own home if he skipped bail. Not anybody else's house."

He started driving the truck back toward the gate. "Somebody from the Range River Police Department will be out here to talk to your father. I have no doubt of that and your father knows it, too. That's why I doubt he's got Jared hiding here. Plus, do you really think Jared would go there? You said it yourself—if the price was right, your father wouldn't hesitate to turn him over to whoever was looking for him. And I'm sure Jared knows that, too. It was a long shot, but I thought it was worth trying. And he said he'd ask around, see if he could get any information." Connor glanced over at Naomi. "All the thugs in town know that Range River Bail Bonds pays for quality information. That might motivate him. And he has a lot of connections."

Greg Santelli motivated by money rather than affection for his children sounded about right.

A thought crossed Naomi's mind, something she hadn't considered before. "Do you think someone might be coming after Jared and me as a way to get back at my dad? For revenge or to blackmail him into committing a crime, something like that? Anyone thinking he was a normal father might believe that hurting Jared and me might somehow hurt him. They might be foolish enough to think they could use threats and attacks against us as leverage."

Connor sighed. "It's possible—but I don't think it's likely. Anyone who knows your dad well enough to try to get something from him would know better than to think he's a loving father. It's not like he pretends to be anything other than what he is. We need to be careful around him. And I don't think you should come back out here. Especially not alone. If it seems like a return visit is a good idea, I'll come back with Danny and Wade."

Looking at Connor's profile, Naomi could see that his jaw muscles were tensed.

Her own stomach was in knots. She'd put up with anything if it would help find Jared, but she couldn't help hoping that nothing about the investigation would force her to cross paths with her father again. He was a part of her history that she was more than willing to leave in the past.

The man beside her, on the other hand...the more time she spent with him, feeling safe and cared for in the shelter of his protection, the harder it was to remember that her feelings for him were supposed to be over and done.

* * *

"This is a good time to go by Jared's apartment," Connor said as they drove through the last bit of forested mountainside before heading into town.

"It is?" Naomi frowned, looking confused. "What makes this a good time? Anything in particular?"

Naomi had been quiet since they'd left her dad's house, her attention fixed on her phone as she appeared to be working her way through messages and emails.

"It's fairly late in the morning," Connor replied. "Which means we're less likely to wake people up if we knock on doors. If you wake somebody from a sound sleep they're less inclined to do you a favor and answer some questions."

Naomi looked up. "You must learn a lot about human nature as a bounty hunter."

More than he wanted to know at times.

"People on the run think they're choosing random actions that will make them difficult to find, but breaking away from routine and old habits is harder than you think. It takes money to skip town and stay away. Fugitives are more likely to stay local, at least at first. Within a few days or weeks, Jared will probably drop by a fast-food place he likes or a grocery store he's used to shopping at. If we know the places he habitually visits we can go to them ahead of time, show the employees there his picture, and offer them a cash reward if they see him and call us. We've found quite a few people that way."

They came to a stop at a red light. Connor looked around for any potential assailant moving toward them. The possibility of a brazen attack in the middle of Range River in broad daylight seemed remote, especially since no one had any reason to know where they were at this precise time, but that didn't make it impossible. They were dealing with professionals, after all.

He glanced again at Naomi, marveling that she could be right here right now, seated beside him. Her dark brown hair, with a few auburn streaks shot through it, was tied up in a high ponytail. Her black-framed glasses gave her a serious appearance that suited her. She'd been so much fun when they were younger, but she'd never been a shallow party girl. Her rough childhood, the way she'd practically had to raise her brother, had forced her into maturity early on.

"Why are you staring at me?" she asked, without looking at him.

Heat spread across his face and he fought

back an embarrassed smile. "I'm not looking at you. I'm looking at the doughnut shop outside your window."

The light turned green and he drove forward. He glanced over after a few moments and it looked like her cheeks were flushed, too. She knew he'd been lying.

Warmth spread through the center of his chest, followed by a dousing of emotional cold water as he reminded himself that she had a life that didn't include him. Or it wouldn't include him any longer once the police found the shooters, cleared Jared and closed the murder investigation.

Determined to do a better job of keeping his emotions under control, Connor made several turns that ultimately took him to a street a couple of blocks from Wolf Lake.

Connor pulled into the parking lot of a small complex with sixteen apartments built in a square around a central courtyard. Someone could sneak undetected in and out of one of the apartments fairly easily if they wanted to. The exterior lighting was modest and Connor didn't spot any security cameras.

"Let's look inside his apartment before you talk to the neighbors," Naomi said as she led the way to her brother's door. "I want to see if anything looks odd. Or if he left behind anything that might hint at where he's gone."

"You're a natural at this." Connor walked behind her, head on a swivel, keeping an eye out for anyone who might be nearby. "Keep in mind that the killers could be here watching the apartment," he added. "Stay alert."

Connor had no doubt the police had come by here last night looking for Jared. If there'd been anything obvious in the apartment pointing to where he'd gone, they would have seen it and taken it. But maybe Naomi would notice something that the police missed because they didn't personally know him.

They reached the door and Connor threw out an arm before Naomi could just barrel inside. "Give me the key and then get behind me."

She nodded and did as he asked.

He reached for the handle and the door easily opened.

"It's already unlocked," Naomi said.

"Stay back." Connor stepped inside, moving slowly and scanning the apartment while listening for signs that someone was in there.

"Hello!" he called out. "Anybody home? Jared? It's Connor."

He moved past the kitchen, glanced at a dirty bowl and spoon in the sink and paper coffee cup from a national chain on the counter. Stepping into the living room, he didn't hear anything to indicate that someone else might be there. But taking things for granted was foolish and dangerous, so he cautiously continued forward until he'd cleared the two bedrooms and the bathroom.

Finally, he breathed a sigh of relief, and lowered the hand that had been hovering near his gun.

He went back to the front door. "No one's here."

"Hard to believe Jared or the police would have left the door unlocked." Naomi stepped inside.

Able to focus on smaller details now, Connor strode through the apartment again, this time glancing around for paper with a name or phone number or address jotted on it. He looked for signs that Jared might have had company recently. He headed for the first bedroom, looking in drawers and closets for signs that Jared had packed clothes and personal items as if he'd planned ahead for a getaway. So far it didn't look that way.

Connor wasn't completely convinced of Jared's innocence. Maybe Jared *had* been forced to point a gun at Kevin and pull the trigger.

But it could also be true that he was involved with the assailants in some other way. Maybe Jared had wanted out and planned to turn the others in, which was why they'd tried to frame him—to destroy his credibility. Jared's walk down the straight and narrow path had started fairly recently. Sometimes people backslid.

"What exactly are we looking for?" Naomi asked.

"We'll know it when we see it," Connor said as he opened the closet of the second bedroom for a closer look and saw a suitcase and duffel bag on the floor. "Maybe nothing."

The front door slammed open.

"Stay here." Connor's heart pounded in his chest, fueled by the fear that he'd led Naomi into danger. "Do you have your phone?" he whispered as he drew his gun and sidestepped toward the doorway, tilting his head to see down the hallway without being seen himself.

"I do," she whispered back, sliding her phone out of her pocket and then looking at him with eyes wide with fear.

"Get ready to call 9-1-1." He glanced toward the window on the bedroom's back wall. "If anything happens, get out through there. But look around before you go out. Make sure there's not already someone waiting for you."

Connor heard the front door close.

He started down the hall, sticking close to the wall and proceeding as quietly as possible.

Someone was in the kitchen.

Connor couldn't be certain it was only one person.

He continued forward, raising his gun just before he made a move that would expose him to anyone who might be waiting in the living room.

No one was there, so it looked like he just had to deal with whoever was in the kitchen.

Connor stepped around the corner, saw the back of a slender man in a T-shirt standing at the sink and called out, "Don't move!"

The man dropped the paper coffee cup in his hand, grabbed a knife from a wooden block on the counter and spun around. "Who are *you*?" he demanded, crouching slightly, one hand raised defensively. "What are you doing here?"

"I'm a bounty hunter, looking for the man who lives here. Jared Santelli."

"I'm looking for him, too." The guy slowly lowered his knife as Connor holstered his weapon.

"I know he's in trouble," the man continued, setting the knife on the counter and righting the paper cup he'd dropped. Connor recognized it as the cup he'd seen when he and Naomi had first arrived. He also spotted a small paper bakery bag on the counter that hadn't been there before.

"I'm in recovery, just like Jared," the young man continued. "He called me three times yesterday but he didn't leave a message. I tried to call him back later but he didn't answer. And then this morning I learned he was in a whole lot of trouble."

"So you figured you'd just come on over and let yourself into his apartment?" Connor asked, skeptical.

"I came to see if he was here. I thought maybe he relapsed and passed out. When I saw he wasn't here, I figured I'd leave him a note for when he did come back. I went out to my car to grab this." He pulled a pen from his pocket. "And my scone." He gestured toward the bag. "Figured if I couldn't find a piece of paper I'd just write on the bag. Let him know I was here. That someone cared enough to come looking for him."

The man's gaze shifted until he was looking past Connor's shoulder. "You must be Jared's sister, Naomi."

"I am."

"Your brother talks about you a lot."

Connor turn to glance at Naomi in time to see her eyes fill with tears.

"Oh, my name's Reg Banks." He offered Naomi a smile that quickly faded. "I'm a friend of Jared's."

"Reg." She paused for a moment. "He's mentioned you."

"So, Reg," Connor interjected, "what can you tell us about Jared that might help us find him? Can you give us the names of some of his friends? Tell us where you think he would hide?"

"He *had* a lot of friends back when he was partying a lot. *Had*." Reg shook his head sadly. "I'd say most of them weren't truly his friends. Not that I knew them personally, I'm just going by what he told me. But if he wanted to get sober, he couldn't hang out with his old partying crowd. And he really wanted to get sober. So he broke off most of those friendships."

"Do you think any of those people would offer him a place to hide if he needed to lie low?" Connor pressed. The best avenue for him to protect Naomi was to find Jared and see if he was somehow the key to ending the attacks on her. Connor would go visit every one of Jared's alleged *friends* if he had to.

"For a price, a few of those people probably would be willing to hide him. But I don't know what money he would have had to offer them. And again, I don't have any names to give you."

"Tell me the truth," Naomi said. "Has my brother turned back to his old habits?"

Reg shook his head. "I haven't seen any signs of that." He glanced down at the coffee that had spilled on the floor when he dropped his cup before adding, "Getting arrested in the drug bust really messed Jared up emotionally. I know he planned to testify against the other guys. There are some drug suppliers in town who are pretty powerful and I'm thinking they'd be willing to do anything they could to stop him."

Connor did his best to assess the situation. Maybe Reg was actually one of the threats but if so, he was a really good liar. Right now, Connor had no way to know.

He exchanged contact information with Reg and after a brief exchange of goodbyes, he hurried Naomi out of there.

SEVEN

"You sure you don't want to go back to the inn for the rest of the day?" Connor glanced at Naomi before pulling out of a strip mall parking lot and heading down the road.

After their stop at Jared's apartment, he'd asked Naomi if she was hungry and she'd told him she was starving. They'd just made a quick stop at a favorite deli in town—where he'd grabbed enough food for the rest of the team after arranging for them to all meet at the Range River Bail Bonds office.

"I want to keep searching for him," Naomi answered after taking a sip of her soda. "And any time I'm not looking for my brother I need to be at my office at Stuart Furniture. My email inbox is bursting. It's not fair to leave it all to James Petrie, my site manager, to handle. I really need to get over there to see what's happening and get a better sense of what needs to be done."

So much for Connor thinking he could get her to hide out while he took care of this case.

"All things considered, I really am okay," Naomi offered after they drove in silence for a few moments. "I handle things a lot better now than I did when I was nineteen. Actually, it's more accurate to say that I do what I can and then I hand the rest over to God. Something I couldn't even fathom back when you and I were together."

A bolt of near panic shot through Connor. This sounded like a lead-up to talking about their past. He could just tell. And he really, *really* didn't want to do that. So he kept his mouth shut.

She laughed after a moment and he glanced over to see her tucking a few tendrils of hair that had fallen free from her ponytail behind her ears. "You don't need to be afraid," she said teasingly.

Seriously? After twenty years apart she could still read him that easily?

"You don't have to talk if you don't want to," she added. "But I will say that one of the many wonderful things I've learned over the past two decades is the ability to face things and talk them out. I resisted at first because it all felt so weird. My family never did that. I know yours didn't, either."

No, they did not talk things out. Not his dad, not his mom, not his stepmom. When there was conflict or things got tense, they drank, clothed themselves in denial and left things unresolved. Connor did that for a long time. Then he found faith, and with it he found a better way to handle things so that his younger siblings could grow up to be emotionally healthy and strong individuals.

But did that mean he needed to go back to his past and dig around in the deepest wound he carried? The one he'd kept secret from his siblings because he just did not want to deal with it? The loss of the unborn child he'd had with Naomi and the absolute meltdown on their marriage?

Nope. He did not need to do that.

"I'm happy for you," he said. It came out sounding borderline sarcastic, which was not how he meant it. But he didn't clarify his intention because he wanted this conversation to end.

"Look," Naomi said after a particularly loud sip of soda. "After we lost the baby, I expected you to fix things that you could not have possibly fixed. It was irrational. I was overwhelmed and I took things out on you. I just want to say I'm sorry."

She'd kept her tone light, but Connor could still hear an echo of pain in her words.

Connor didn't trust himself to respond. Maybe he'd break down. If there was anything worth crying about, it was the loss of his child, but he didn't know how to let go like that— even when he wanted to. If he weren't trapped in this moving vehicle he would have already walked away. Quickly. And he couldn't help wondering if Naomi knew that and had timed this conversation on purpose.

Finally, feeling like he had to say *something*, he cleared his throat. "If there's one thing I learned raising Danny and Hayley it's that you do the best you can. If you make a mistake you pray about it, let it go and try to do better the next time."

"You're not going to accept my apology?" she said softly.

He shook his head. "That's not what I meant." He sighed heavily. "Look, we were young. Neither of us knew what we were doing. Let's just leave it at that."

He glanced around as they waited at a traffic light. Part of him actually hoped someone would try to attack them right now. Fighting was something he knew how to do. Something he was comfortable with. Was that a good thing? Sometimes he wasn't sure. But he'd done what he could to put his skills to good use catching bad guys.

They made it to the office without further conversation, which was a relief.

Connor grabbed the bags of food and Naomi got the drinks.

When they walked into the bail bonds office, Hayley caught his eye, glanced at Naomi, and then looked at him again with a smirk and a lifting of her eyebrows.

Connor growled in response and his little sister quickly dropped the smirk and looked away.

As they were getting settled to begin their meal, Naomi got a phone call.

"My father," she said before tapping the screen.

Connor moved close beside her, aware of a flush of warmth on his face and neck at the nearness of her. He did his best to direct his attention away from the lavender scent of her hair. "Put it on speaker."

"Hi," Naomi said as she answered the call.

Connor hated to see that familiar look of

uncertainty and fear on her face. When they were kids she'd been determined to overcome her fear of her father and his violent outbursts, but he wasn't surprised to see it lingered.

"Yeah. You got any money available to pay people for information about your brother?" Greg Santelli asked, not bothering with a greeting for his daughter or any friendly chit-chat. "I know cops and bounty hunters sometimes do that. It is for your little brother, after all. He and I haven't been as financially fortunate as you."

Connor ground his teeth. The odds were good that Greg Santelli would just pocket any money he was given.

"I can provide some money for that," Naomi said.

"That's my girl. How much?"

"Depends on the quality of the information."

Connor detected a new note of confidence in her tone. Good for her.

The conversation wrapped up very quickly after that. Once she'd disconnected, Naomi turned to Connor. "Do you believe he'll really try to help find Jared or do you think he'll lie to me for the money?"

Connor didn't know, so he shrugged. It sounded like Naomi still carried a little bit of hope that her father would turn into a decent human being someday.

Hayley and her husband, Jack, sat together at one desk. Danny and Wade sat at another. While everyone ate, Connor started a recap of the trip to see Naomi's father followed by the visit to Jared's apartment and the unexpected arrival of Reg. He and Naomi had knocked on the neighboring apartment doors before they left, hoping to get some additional information, but no one had answered.

"We've got an informant to meet with in about forty-five minutes," Hayley said with a glance at the other bounty hunters. "It's one of my regulars, who claims he's heard people talk about one of your attackers—Sergio Almada. Maybe that will give us some direction on where to start looking for him."

"Good." For Naomi's sake, Connor wanted to find Jared because that was *her* biggest concern. But the truth was he was especially focused on finding the professional killers, Almada and his partner, Ladd Olsen. They were the biggest threats to Naomi, obviously. He was working under the assumption that it was them who'd tried to kill Naomi with the explosion at her home last night.

They were discussing possible ways to find

all three of their fugitives when Naomi's phone rang. It was right after Connor had mentioned wanting to visit the landscaping company where Jared was employed.

"Sounds like a good idea," Naomi said before setting down her sandwich and looking at her phone's screen. "James Petrie," she murmured with a glance at Connor. "Excuse me, it's a work call. I need to take this."

She politely stepped away to take the call, but she didn't go so far that Connor couldn't hear her. It sounded like her site manager was calling with a list of things she needed to address. She reassured him that she would come by the office to take care of them right away.

"I'm going to need to go into work," she said after the call ended. "Today's Friday. They're waiting for me to get there and give them some direction on what to do first thing Monday morning before they cut out for the weekend."

"Okay, I'll take you there," Connor said.

"Maybe you could drop me off, go talk to Jared's employer and coworkers, and then come back and get me." She shook her head. "I don't want to waste time. I want to find my brother, but I've got to take care of my business. I can't let down my employees."

"All right. I'll drive you to work, check

things out, and if it looks okay I'll drop you off and then come back to pick you up in a couple of hours." It might be easier to just call Jared's employer and talk to them on the phone, but years of experience had taught him that he was less likely to get useful information that way. People were more likely to open up if he spoke to them face-to-face.

Connor wasn't thrilled about having Naomi out of his sight. But the more quickly they got answers, the sooner she'd be safe.

Naomi clicked the "confirm order" button then closed the tab and took a deep breath. After a little over an hour she was nearly at the end of the action list she'd created in response to James's concerns.

It had been difficult to concentrate when she'd first sat at her desk. Fear that Jared wasn't just running from the law but that he'd been captured by the bad guys was never far from her mind. But eventually she'd forced herself to focus and she'd gotten some work done.

"So, are we going to be okay on the hardware supplies?" James asked, sticking his head through the open office door, hanging on to the frame for a moment before finally stepping all the way in.

A heavyset man with thinning graying hair and a neatly trimmed beard to match, he had worked at Stuart Furniture since he was a young man. His dedication to his job was obvious, and it was one of the reasons Naomi had taken the plunge and bought the business. There were several people on staff who put their heart into their work, crafting tables and chairs, dressers and chests of drawers, standing mirror frames and bookcases and curio cabinets.

"Yep, I ordered everything," Naomi told him. "We've got hinges and latches and shelf supports and drawer pulls and all sorts of things coming. Express delivery, in fact." They sourced much of their lumber locally so they had a fair amount of that on hand, but a lot of the accoutrements had to be ordered in. "I've got some wood stain and varnish set up to be delivered on Monday."

James pretended to wipe sweat from his brow before smiling broadly. "Thanks." His smile faltered. "I know you have other things on your mind. And I'm sorry to bug you with this stuff but we really can't function without it."

"I know. I'll get you set up to make purchases yourself as soon as I have time." He'd had more latitude before, but all the previously existing accounts had been shut down with the transfer of the business to her new ownership.

"Speaking of the stain and varnish, let me go check the storage closet and make sure we're following all the proper rules for our chemicals. It's the last thing on my to-do list for now." Several of the items stored on the premises were volatile. Not only did she want to avoid fires or someone being harmed by fumes, but she also knew from prior experience that governmental safety agencies could show up at any time to conduct an audit.

James nodded. "We do need to get on that. It's just one more of the things that were left undone as Mr. Berger fell ill and things stopped running as smoothly. We lost a lot of employees who were afraid the business was going to go under." Huntley Berger's grandfather had started the business. Huntley's own children had launched careers in other directions and weren't interested in taking over the factory. He'd kept it going as long as he could, but had finally been forced to put it up for sale. "I can take care of it if you want to go ahead and leave," James said.

She kind of *did* want to leave. Connor was a bounty hunter with experience and an excellent reputation; he certainly didn't need her help. But she still believed in her theory that if Jared saw her out and about looking for him, he might be more likely to turn himself in.

Naomi stood and stretched her back. "That's okay, I'll do it." It shouldn't take that long. She grabbed a tablet with an outdated inventory of items plus proper safety guidelines so she could make adjustments to the way the chemicals were stored if need be. "You can go ahead and go home if you want," she told James.

"Nah. I've still got six people working. Some of the supplies they needed to complete their projects came in this morning. They're paid by the hour and they're earning overtime so they aren't complaining."

"All right." Naomi headed out and walked through the shop, a cavernous area with a concrete floor and high roof. The roll doors were closed due to the chilly weather, which made the echoing sounds of sanders and hammers and power drills all the louder.

She didn't mind the noise. It reminded her of the days when she'd worked with Matt. Her heart squeezed at the thought of him. He'd been a good-natured man who loved the outdoors and loved to make things. He'd grown up in a much more functional family than her own and from them she'd learned a lot about faith, about resolving conflicts without getting violent and about how to run a business. She and Matt had dreamed of having children to add to their happy life, but it had never happened.

After chatting with a few of the employees she resumed walking. She wove her way through aisles of metal racks holding finished projects and raw lumber. This side of the facility was shadowy and quiet since most of the workers had already left for the day.

She noted the placard on the storage room door warning of the chemicals stored inside. She unlocked the door and stepped in. A small, high window let in the waning afternoon light, making the thick dust motes stirred by her opening the door hard to ignore. She flipped on the single light bulb in the ceiling and began reading the labels on the shelves. At some point in the past someone had tried to group things correctly, but the organization had clearly fallen apart.

She'd begun comparing things to her inventory list when she heard a sound behind her. She was in a corner of the L-shaped room where she couldn't see the door. "James? Is that you?"

She heard a whoosh sound just before the

overhead light went out. And then she saw flames. Startled, she jumped up from the work stool where she'd been sitting, toppling it over.

There was a second whoosh, and this time, she saw the explosive hit the floor, sending shards of glass and flammable liquid everywhere. The accelerant pooled with flames hovering over it.

The door slammed shut.

Someone was trying to kill her again. And this time, there was no refrigerator door to hide behind, or icy rain to put out the flames. Most of all, there was no Connor to run to her side. She was alone. Trapped. And she was about to die.

It was already hot in the small room—more of a closet, really—and the acrid smell of the chemicals from the accelerant burned her lungs as she tried to breathe the smoky, heated air.

She looked overhead, the lights from the flames illuminating the ceiling, certain that she would see a fire sprinkler.

She didn't.

What a time to notice that particular safety feature was missing.

She glanced around for an alarm pull but didn't see one.

Fighting back panic, she patted her pockets hoping she'd brought her phone with her.

Her heart soared when she found it in her back pocket and pulled it out. She frantically punched in 9-1-1 and got…nothing. The walls were thick cement. The facility was on the edge of town at the base of a substantial hill. A single bar of connectivity flickered on and off.

"Help!" The scream rose up from deep inside of her, the effort grating her already sore throat and increasingly tight lungs. *"Help!"*

On the shelves around her, metal cans of various chemical solvents made groaning and popping sounds as the heat caused the containers to expand. Already, some of the plastic containers were softening and starting to slump.

In moments all of the chemicals would start to mix together and she'd be forced to breathe in the toxic fumes. That would be enough to kill her, if the flames or lack of oxygen didn't get to her first.

Panic made it even harder to breathe. *Think!*

Some of the storage shelving was wood instead of metal, yet another mistake of safety protocol, she noted, a little hysterically.

Stop! She forced herself to shake off the creeping sense of hopelessness crawling up her spine. She'd fought off that sensation in her life before. More than once. She would not let it drag her down now.

The sound of a person pounding on the door felt like someone had thrown her a lifeline.

"Naomi!" It was James.

"Here!" She only got out the single word before she was wracked by a coughing fit.

Flames still shimmered across the accelerant spilled all over the floor like a burning lake. She would have to get through them to get to the door after James opened it. Unless James had brought a fire extinguisher with him.

"Someone's jammed something in the keyhole." James's voice sounded muffled. "I need to get a crowbar."

That would take time she didn't have. It was getting hotter and the air felt thinner. The chemicals made her dizzy and nauseous. She was afraid she might faint.

A wooden case collapsed into a burning pile of rubble in front of the door, splashing the accelerant and sending flames up along the shelving as its contents fell.

Naomi burst into tears. She couldn't help it. The resolve she'd managed to summon up moments ago had simply vanished.

She'd pushed so hard to stay strong ever since seeing poor Kevin Ashton's lifeless body. She'd prayed and managed to hold it together after her brother disappeared and then her house was bombed. She'd even managed to push back the old fears that had resurfaced when she saw her father.

But this was too much. She was so tired and confused and her knees were getting wobbly. She'd fought to hold herself together and now she'd had enough of fighting.

Where was James with the crowbar?

Lord, help!

She looked around at the smoke and the eerie glow, wondering if this was the last thing she was going to ever see. But then her eyes caught on something.

The window. It was narrow and high up. There was a metal screen over it. But it was the best option she had. If she somehow got up there, she could open the screen if it had a latch—or break it open if it didn't—and get some air. Maybe she could get connectivity for her phone.

She managed to use some of the metal shelving to climb up until she had one foot on a shelf and another on the concrete window ledge. Remarkably, the window had a latch. But when she tried to squeeze it to get the window open, it wouldn't budge. It looked like it hadn't been opened in a long time. Maybe never.

Her eyes were watery with tears, both from

crying and from the smoke and toxic fumes. She felt shaky where she was perched, like she wouldn't be able to manage her balance much longer.

Groaning with the effort, she tried the latch again. Fueled by desperation, she finally got it to move and she slid the window open.

The cool air she breathed in felt like a shock to her system. For a moment it almost felt as if she was taking in too much oxygen, to the point where it was overwhelming her.

The feeling was quickly extinguished when the fire was fed by the new source of oxygen and dark smoke from the fire began to rush toward her face as it rolled out the window.

She pushed at the screen, thinking she would rather jump and risk the injury from the drop down to the hard-packed dirt outside than stay inside with the poisonous fumes and fire. But the screen wouldn't budge. It had been bolted to the concrete wall by a person obviously more concerned with a potential thief trying to break into the building than someone trying to escape from it.

Naomi kicked at the screen out of sheer frustration.

In the twilight outside, she saw vehicle headlights turn into the parking lot at the opposite end of the facility.

Emergency response for the fire? Her spirits soared with hope and then dropped when she realized the headlights were too small to be from a fire engine.

Through the smoke still pouring out the window, she saw the vehicle stop, and then accelerate in her direction.

When it got closer she could see it was Connor.

Seconds later, he was outside his truck and looking up at the window. "Naomi?"

"I'm trapped in here!" she screamed out the window, fingers pressing through the openings in the metal screen as she tried again to break it free. "I can't get the screen off. It's bolted on."

She watched Connor run and grab a tow chain from the cargo box in the back of his truck. He attached one end of the chain to the truck's trailer hitch. He held on to the other end as he climbed up onto the cab of his truck so that he could reach the window. When he got there he used a couple of carabiners to attach the free end of the chain to the window screen. "It's going to be okay," he said, working quickly. "When you see me get into the truck, back away from the screen. I don't know what'll happen when I pull this loose. Some of the surrounding wall might crumble onto you."

In an instant he'd returned to the truck.

Naomi moved back, but not very far. The stream of fresh air coming in through the window was the only thing keeping her conscious.

Connor hit the gas and the heavy screen bowed and whined and twisted before it finally popped off.

He backed up alongside the building until the truck's cab was under the window again, and clambered back up to help Naomi, who was already halfway out of the window.

"I've got you," he said as she climbed the rest of the way out of the new opening, and he took her in his arms. In the distance, she finally heard the sirens she'd been listening for.

She buried herself in Connor's embrace, her head pressed against his chest, engulfed with relief at the feel of his arms wrapped around her body. At the same time, her pounding heart and painful lungs reminded her that she wasn't really safe, and she wouldn't be until they found whoever was so determined to kill her.

EIGHT

Connor sat in his office at the inn looking at Naomi and mentally beating himself up over the fact that he'd nearly gotten her killed. He should not have left her unprotected. He should have stayed at Stuart Furniture with her while she got her work done.

"It's not your fault," she said in a voice made gravelly by the smoke she'd been forced to inhale.

Connor lifted a brow in response, not especially surprised at this point that she could guess what he was thinking. But she was wrong to let him off the hook so easily.

"Obviously I survived," she added. "And I'm grateful that you showed up in time."

Connor was grateful, too. *Thank You, Lord.*

The fire engine and an ambulance had arrived on scene right after Naomi was pulled out of the building. Remarkably, she hadn't suffered any serious burns. She'd accepted the oxygen mask the paramedic had offered, but refused a ride with him to the emergency room. She'd wanted Connor to drive her to the hospital, instead. At the moment, it looked like she'd escaped any serious damage from the fumes she'd inhaled, but the doctor had directed her to monitor any headaches or dizziness. They'd just arrived at the inn a few minutes ago. The bounty hunters, along with Wade's wife, Charlotte, had been there to greet them.

"Have you gotten any information from the police?" Wade asked. His wife sat beside him, their hands entwined. "Any follow-up?"

Connor felt a stab of envy, wishing he could be sitting beside Naomi, holding her hand, offering her the reassurance he knew she wanted. Once she was outside the building and safe from the fire, she'd wrapped her arms around him and clutched him tightly. He'd returned the embrace, grateful she was alive. After a few moments he'd held her at arm's length, asked if she had any injuries and taken a quick scan to reassure himself that she was okay.

Convinced that she didn't need immediate medical care, he'd wrapped his arms around her again, felt her shaking and crying. He'd held her as long as she'd wanted, waiting for her to break the embrace. When she finally did, he'd felt like a part of himself had been broken away.

Which was ridiculous.

Still, when they'd walked into the den that served as his office, he'd intentionally headed for his desk chair rather than one of the sofas. He didn't trust himself to sit beside her without reaching for her hand or wrapping his arm around her shoulders. Partly to comfort her, but also to reassure himself that she was okay.

And maybe because he loved the feeling of holding her again. Even under such dire circumstances. And despite the fact that she'd made it clear years ago that their relationship was over. So it wasn't like they had a chance at a future. Even if he wanted one. Which he didn't.

Connor shook his head in response to Wade's question. "I haven't spoken to the police since we left the factory to go to the hospital. I messaged Detective Romanov while Naomi was seeing the doctor. She said she'd get back to me sometime tonight."

Naomi had described to the police what she'd experienced. Connor hoped the facility would have security footage that would help explain the chain of events.

"I want to know if James is okay," Naomi said. "He went to get a crowbar to force open the door and after that I don't know what happened to him."

Connor wanted to know what happened to him, too. It was probably unfair of Connor to expect Naomi's employee to look out for her under such extreme circumstances. The guy was experienced in furniture manufacturing. He wasn't a security expert. Still, what was his story regarding his whereabouts during the fire? Why hadn't he done more to save her once he'd realized she was trapped?

"I never got a chance to ask you, what did you learn about Jared at his workplace?" Naomi said.

In the tumult of giving their reports to the responding police at the furniture company and then going to the ER, they hadn't had time to talk about much else. The ride back to the inn had been quiet, with Connor's attention constantly shifting between the road ahead and what he could see reflected in the mirrors as he kept an eye out for yet another attack.

"Sounds like your brother had really gotten his act together and was doing a good job,"

Connor answered, happy to give her a little bit of good news. "They'd had absolutely no problems with him and no complaints from customers."

Jared's heavy drinking had caused multiple problems at his previous jobs, typically causing him to get fired or to walk off in an angry fit.

Maybe he really had changed.

"What about the other two? The killers, Almada and Olsen," she said with a glance toward the bounty hunters seated on the sofas. "Has anyone learned anything about them?" Her gaze settled on Hayley. "Weren't you supposed to meet someone who would tell you about Sergio Almada?"

"We learned that he and Olsen have worked together as a team in Range River, back before they went to Vegas. They were hired by big-money criminals to kill or scare off competitors. The word is that they're good at what they do. They don't leave witnesses or clues behind, which is why the cops don't know much about them. Yeah, they have arrest records, but very few convictions."

"They typically work for people who solve their own problems and don't call the cops for help when there's trouble," Hayley's husband, Jack, added. He lifted his eyebrows slightly as he focused on Naomi. "It seems to me like they underestimated you and your brother and got careless. Assumed you'd freeze up in fear and be easy to pick off since neither of you are hardened criminals."

An unnerving image of Naomi lying dead alongside her brother on the grass behind Kevin's house slithered into Connor's thoughts and he quickly shook it off. Instead, he shifted his focus to gratitude that Naomi had had her wits about her and had managed to evade the shooters and get herself and Jared to safety.

His phone chimed and he glanced down at the screen. "Detective Romanov is here." He went to let her in and after a brief greeting to everyone in Connor's office, she took a seat. One of Connor's cats, a tortoiseshell named Layla who'd previously showed a fondness for the detective, sat in front of her chair and stared at her until Romanov patted her legs and the cat jumped up to settle in her lap.

"How are you feeling?" Romanov asked Naomi. "I had a look inside that storage closet after the fire was out. It looked and smelled awful—and that was with the window open and the flames put out. It must have been pretty horrific when the fire was raging."

"I'll be okay." Naomi's voice was still

scratchy. "I just really want to find my brother and put a stop to all of this."

Romanov nodded. "We want that, too. I read the reports written by the first officers on scene. But there are a few things I want to ask you myself. Even if that means you'll be repeating yourself."

"Of course."

"Did you see or hear anybody before the fire started and you were trapped inside?"

Naomi shook her head, wincing slightly. "The only person I heard during the whole incident was James Petrie, my site manager. He tried to get me out, but he couldn't get the door open. He said he was going to get a crowbar, but I don't know what happened after that. I guess it took him a while to find one and by then Connor had arrived and helped me to get outside."

"Petrie got struck on the head from behind. Knocked unconscious. Presumably by the same person who started the fire."

Connor was watching Naomi closely and he saw her eyes tear up.

"What have you picked up off security video?" Connor asked the detective.

Romanov shook her head. "Not much. Some of those cameras probably stopped functioning years ago. Things really did fall apart as Mr. Berger became ill and regular maintenance fell by the wayside. Bottom line, we caught very vague images of one or two individuals in the parking lot that we haven't yet identified."

Romanov gave the cat a couple of pats before turning her attention back to the bounty hunters. "What have you got to share with me?"

Connor gave her a summary of what his team had learned during the day. She made note of Reg Banks's name after hearing about his appearance at Jared's apartment and then turned her attention to Naomi. "What's your dad's relationship with your brother? I need an honest assessment. We're aware of your father's extensive criminal history. Obviously. I had a couple of officers go interview him today. Do you think your brother could have been working with your dad and then turned on him?"

"No." Naomi blew out a breath and shook her head. "I don't think Jared was working with my dad. And as far as their relationship goes, well, I don't know exactly."

Connor saw fear in her eyes despite her protestations. He suspected she wanted to believe Jared knew better than to get involved with anything their father had a hand in…but she couldn't be sure.

"You heard Connor's report." Naomi's voice sounded almost pleading. "Jared's been going to work. Doing well. He's not involved in anything illegal anymore. And if he was, he'd know better than to work with our father."

"Okay," Romanov said neutrally.

"What about disgruntled employees at the furniture factory?" Danny asked. "Could there be something there to pursue? Was there somebody else who wanted to buy it but they lost out to you and now they're holding a grudge?"

"The business was about to close," Naomi said. "I bought it to keep people working. The response I've gotten from all of the employees has been uniformly positive. Frankly, I think they're all relieved to still have jobs. I haven't come across a single instance of hostility or any kind of trouble until the fire today. As far as a competitor for buying the factory goes, there was only one other person who made an offer on it and I've never heard any kind of outcry from him. It's not like there was a bidding war."

Danny shrugged. "Could there be something on the property of value? Maybe something hidden that someone wants to get to?"

He shook his head. "I don't know how any of that would lead to the murder of Kevin and the earlier attacks on Naomi and her brother. I'm just throwing out ideas here."

"I suppose it could be worth the time to look around the facility and the surrounding property," Hayley mused. "See if we find anything interesting. But the fire today could just be an attack of opportunity. It might not mean that the attacks overall are connected to the business. It's where Naomi works so it would make sense that someone looking to get to her would assume that she'd show up there eventually. Anybody taking a look at the dilapidated state of the place could guess that security wasn't great."

"If we get any information indicating a specific direction we should investigate, I'll let you know," Romanov said. She gave the cat a few more pats on the head before setting her on the ground and then standing up. "We'll be interviewing all the employees to find out if they saw anything or anyone unusual." She headed for the door. "Keep me posted on what you learn. I'll update you with whatever information I'm willing to release." The words sounded a little harsh, but Connor understood that many of the facts the detective obtained during an investigation had to be kept under wraps.

He walked her to the door, and when he came back, Naomi and his team members were all on their feet. It was getting late. Everyone was tired.

"Where could we look next?" Naomi asked. "I know you'll be pressing your informants and that sort of thing, but what can *I* help with?"

"You can get some rest and take care of yourself," Connor said.

She looked at him for a moment and smiled. His heart warmed. "Maybe we actually should talk to the other guy who tried to buy the business, Tyler Copley, and see if he knows anything," she suggested. "I was a little surprised that he didn't come back with a counteroffer. Maybe he heard something about the business or the employees or something that made him back out."

"Like what?" Hayley asked.

Naomi shrugged. "I don't have any theories. I don't know that the attacks are directly related to the furniture company. I just want to do everything I can to find Jared." She shook her head as if to clear her thoughts. "I'm tired and maybe I'm just grasping at straws."

"We never know where a pivotal bit of information will come from," Hayley said. "I think it's worth pursuing every possible line of inquiry until something turns into a solid lead."

Connor nodded. "Agreed. Let's see if we can get an interview with Tyler Copley tomorrow."

"I've got his contact information," Naomi said, her voice sounding faint.

"We've done all we can for now." Connor turned to her. "Why don't you go get some rest?"

While she slept he would stay up and review Jared's file. He'd also compose a message to shoot out to fellow bounty hunters in the region asking for their help. Perhaps one of them had gone hunting for Almada or Olsen in the past and they'd gathered some details about them that could be helpful to Connor and his team now. After that he would do anything and everything else he could think of to help with the case.

"I believe I am going to turn in," Naomi said. After offering a general good-night to everyone, she walked out of the den toward the stairs.

"All right, I know everyone has other cases they're working on," Connor said once she was out of earshot, not wanting her concerned about being a burden on his team. "What updates do you have for me on those?"

His crew gave their reports on the other bail-jumping cases they were working on.

"I know chasing down Jared and looking for Almada and Olsen are taking up a lot of your time," Connor said.

"Don't worry about it," Danny interjected before he could continue. "We'll get everything taken care of." Connor's younger brother offered a signature dazzling smile before glancing in the direction where Naomi had disappeared. "Everybody understands how important this is to you."

The message was clear. They realized how important *Naomi* was to him. He might as well admit—at least to himself—that he did care about her. Still. And it wasn't just the stab of nostalgia he'd felt when she'd first spoken to him on the phone. It was an attraction to who she was in the here and now.

The inner core was the same woman he'd fallen in love with so long ago. But in some ways she'd grown and changed. Time, experience and her faith journey had refined and strengthened her into someone even more wonderful than she'd been before. Could he have changed, too, without realizing it, for the better?

Had she noticed or did she even care?

He shook off the emotions that were of no practical use right now. "Plan on working hard until we find Jared as well as the two shooters." He barked the words like orders and made sure he was wearing his game face.

There was no room for emotion here. There was only room for determination. Even with the lousy security and shadowy interior, the attack at the furniture company had been risky and bold. Whoever wanted Naomi dead was willing to take increasing risks. The cops were doing their best, but it was Connor and his team who were guarding Naomi and it was becoming increasingly challenging to keep her alive.

"You sure you don't want to stay here at the inn today?" Connor slipped on his heavy denim jacket and flipped up the collar. "I know the fire yesterday took a lot out of you."

Naomi fought to keep the expression on her face neutral. *Of course* she didn't want to hide out here while her brother was potentially in danger. Or at least ruining his future by running from the law instead of facing justice. But she realized Connor was just expressing concern for her safety so she held back on the sharp response forming on the tip of her tongue. "I still want to help look for him," she said with as much calmness as she could muster. "I got several hours of solid sleep last night and I'm doing a lot better this morning."

He didn't argue with her as she wrapped a knit scarf around her neck and stuffed her gloves into her coat pocket. The weather was expected to be dry today, but temperatures would dip below freezing. The first significant snowstorm of the season was predicted to make its way down from the Gulf of Alaska within the next couple of days. Naomi didn't need to be a bounty hunter to realize that once serious winter weather settled in it would be harder to get leads on Jared's whereabouts. When snow and ice covered the area, people hunkered down indoors. The odds of someone seeing her brother out and about would drop considerably.

"So, are you guys ready to work through the list of possible contacts for Sergio Almada and Ladd Olsen?" Connor asked his crew during their morning meeting. Hayley and Danny each sipped coffee with an eye on their brother, while Jack and Wade both glanced at tablets, taking a look at information that Connor had forwarded to them. He'd gotten Almada and

Olsen's bail bondsman to send him copies of their files and he'd come up with a few ideas for his crew to pursue.

Hayley nodded. "We'll start with Almada's former neighbors and employers and go from there."

"Make sure you keep me updated. Naomi and I are going to meet with an informant who contacted me last night. He says he wants to talk about Jared." Connor offered Naomi a slight shrug. He'd told her about the possible lead first thing this morning. "We'll see if he actually knows anything helpful or if he's just trying to get some money out of me."

"What about the fire last night?" Danny asked, with a glance at Naomi. "Do you have any leads to follow from that? Maybe talk to Detective Romanov this morning and see if she learned anything new that could help us find Almada and Olsen? Because I'm going to go out on a limb here and assume that either they were involved in setting that fire or they're connected to whoever set the fire. They might have hired someone."

"Maybe they paid one of the employees," Hayley added.

"I'll talk to my manager about that later today," Naomi said. "Right now I want to give him time to rest and recover. Meanwhile, I called the other guy who was interested in buying the furniture company and left a message asking him to call me. I thought I did my due diligence before making an offer on the property but maybe I missed something and the guy, Tyler, can fill me in on it."

The dogs got underfoot as everyone made their way to the foyer and out the door. Naomi didn't miss Connor's efforts to give each of the four canines a goodbye pat on the head. The cats had gone their separate ways a while ago, although two of them remained nearby curled together on a club chair by the fireplace and close to Maribel, who sat on a sofa with an open laptop, getting some administrative work done.

Naomi squinted in the bright sunlight as she stepped outside. The sky was a brilliant blue without a cloud in sight—the way it always seemed to be just ahead of a significant storm.

Connor opened the truck door for her and she slid inside. He drove them toward the west side of town. "You feeling all right?" he asked.

His constant checking to see if she was okay brought Naomi back to how it was when they were married and she was pregnant. Such a short segment of her life—the time from when she first found out she was pregnant to the moment when it was all over—and yet it loomed so large in her memories. Even after all these years. Thinking of it brought back a fragile, sweet and sad press of emotion.

"If I inhaled enough smoke and chemicals to do any damage yesterday I think I'd know it by now," she said. Plus the blood samples they'd drawn while she was in the emergency room hadn't indicated anything alarming. "I'm fine, really." The sensation of a scratchy throat had almost disappeared by now.

"Okay. I'll try to stop worrying." A slight self-conscious smile played across Connor's lips. And then almost immediately the smile hardened into a tight line. He was keeping an eye on the road ahead of him, but also regularly checking out their surroundings through the windows along with his side and rearview mirrors. Always vigilant. And with good reason. Naomi might be okay right now, but she'd nearly gotten killed last night. And she had no reason to believe the attacker or attackers would hesitate to try to get at her again.

What strange and unpredictable turns her and Connor's lives had taken. Especially these last few days.

"How come you never got married again?"

Naomi clapped her hand over her mouth. She hadn't intended to voice what she'd been thinking but the words just slipped out.

Connor tensed. Naomi could see his shoulders stiffen and his jaw clench.

She didn't blame him. She had no right to ask him something that personal. Not when they were all but strangers to one another at this point. If they were becoming friends after twenty years apart, then this new friendship was starting from scratch. And she'd just overstepped her bounds.

"I'm sorry I asked," she said quickly. "Never mind. It's none of my business. I was just… thinking about the old days." She fumbled with the words, taken off guard by the emotion that gripped her when she said them. "That's why I asked."

She didn't want him to jump to the conclusion that she was asking because she had a romantic interest in him. *She didn't.*

Okay, *she wasn't going to let herself* develop an interest in him. And that was almost the same thing. Wasn't it? Too much time had passed. She *still* didn't want to be married to a man who wouldn't talk out his thoughts and feelings with her. Obviously they were a terrible match—they'd been married and gotten *divorced.* He was supposed to be part of her past—someone from a relationship she had moved beyond.

"I was so busy trying to figure out how to take care of Danny and Hayley for the first few years after our dad and their mom died that I didn't have time for a personal life," Connor finally said, surprising Naomi. She'd assumed he'd either ignore the question or brush her off with a vague answer.

He steered the truck along the winding road. There were thick stands of trees on either side and Naomi found herself peering into the shadows, half expecting to see a shooter positioned in there with a gun pointed at her. She'd had dreams the last couple of nights filled with assailants jumping out at her and trying to grab her. She'd awoken with a jittery, paranoid sensation and that same feeling was demanding her attention right now.

Connor rubbed a hand over his freshly shaved cheeks and chin. His aftershave smelled like cedar and a cozy spice. Nutmeg, maybe.

Naomi felt edgy, but the scent and the man wearing it beside her made her feel grounded enough that she could resist losing herself in anxiety and fear.

"Dating when I finally had time for it didn't

go all that well for me," Connor added a few moments later. "Raising Danny and Hayley was stressful. I didn't know what I was doing and I was afraid I'd ruin their lives. I carried that anxiety with me everywhere—even on dates. As you can imagine, that didn't go over well. But I was so focused on my homelife—and so convinced that I was going to mess it up—that I barely even noticed when the women lost interest. I was too busy spiraling. Eventually, after a lot of prodding, I agreed to visit Still Waters Church with Maribel because I was desperate for hope and direction. She'd been attending services there for about six months at that point.

"Best decision I ever made. I came to faith and that in turn changed the way I lived my life. Including dating. I was able to pay more attention to it than I had before—but that meant that I was more aware when things weren't working. I met several nice women who were very good people but I just knew we were not headed for marriage and it seemed wrong to keep dating them. So I ended the relationships." He sighed heavily. "I had no doubt it was in their best interests as well as mine. We both know I'm not good husband material, anyway."

He glanced over at Naomi with a wry grin and she felt her heart break. She was certain she was the reason he thought that about himself. Because in the middle of everything, when she was so heartbroken over losing the baby and he didn't have anything to say about it, she'd told him he was a bad husband.

The memory made her want to kick herself.

"That's not true," she said softly. "And I'm sorry for the harsh, unfair things I said to you before we went our separate ways." A feeling of tightness that she could not blame on smoke inhalation last night settled in her throat. It was regret, pure and simple. Regret at her own behavior. "I was too young back then to understand that people process things in different ways," she finally managed to say. And then she shook her head. "Wait, I don't want to make excuses for myself. I just want to say that I was wrong. You would make the right woman a great husband."

They reached the end of the forested section of road. The view opened up to a section of widely spaced houses with lawns, and after that they approached an area with shops and bars and restaurants.

"Matt and I wanted children but it just didn't happen," Naomi added. She'd pushed Connor to talk about a very personal topic and now it seemed only fair that she reveal something emotionally intimate, too. "We talked about consulting a doctor and getting something started with fertility treatments, but we were so busy with building our company that we kept putting it off. We kept saying that we were not quite to the point where we could afford to take time away from work to lavish attention on a child. Or children." She took a deep breath when her voice was about to break. "And then he starting getting sick, and the next thing I knew, he was gone."

"I'm so sorry that happened to you," Connor said gently.

She sat up straighter, determined to get her emotions under control. "Well, I suppose nobody's life goes exactly according to plan."

Connor slowed the truck and parked in front of a corner sandwich shop. "The name of the informant we're going to meet here is Pete Slack. He doesn't have a history of violent crimes and I've never had any trouble with him. But some people can be tempted to do anything for the right amount of money. The possibility exists that this is some kind of a setup, so keep your eyes open and stay close to me."

They got out of the truck and he protectively took hold of her arm as they reached the sidewalk. "Ready?"

Naomi nodded. Her life had reached the bizarre point where she had to be cautious walking into a neighborhood sandwich shop. But she would do what she had to, because not being vigilant could end her life.

NINE

Connor spotted Pete sitting at a table in the corner with a paper coffee cup and partially eaten breakfast sandwich in front of him. With his spiky hair and baggy, faded T-shirt, he looked like a kid. But he was almost thirty. He had lived a rough life from the time he got kicked out of his parents' house as a teenager, and he'd become an informant for Connor when the bounty hunter tracked him down after he skipped a court date. The big brother, tough-love-type advice that Connor had given him hadn't been enough to turn Pete's life around, but Pete had appreciated the effort.

Pete still battled addiction issues and his alcohol-fueled crimes ran the gamut from petty theft to breaking and entering unoccupied homes. He'd never hurt anyone, but Connor couldn't count on that continuing to be the case.

Connor gave Pete a nod in greeting and then gestured toward a table near the wall. "Over there." Connor didn't want Naomi sitting by a window. He also wanted to take his seat in a location where he could watch anyone entering or exiting through either of the two doors visible in the dining area.

"You don't have to talk to Pete if he makes you uncomfortable," Connor said quietly as he pulled out a chair for her. The bounty hunter would sit on the outside chair so that anyone attempting to approach Naomi would have to get through him first.

"I'll talk to him," Naomi said. "That's why I came along. To see if I can help push things forward and find Jared. This has already gone on way too long."

"I agree." The daring attempt on Naomi yesterday made it clear the people who were after her were getting desperate. The chances were good that the attacks would start coming at a faster rate.

"What's up?" Pete swaggered over with his coffee and partially eaten breakfast sandwich and sat down across from Connor. He cast a curious glance toward Naomi.

"I'm here to listen to what you have to tell me," Connor said, then he introduced Naomi.

"Oh wow, Jared's sister. He talks about you a lot. He really looks up to you."

Naomi looked like she was blinking back tears. When she didn't respond after a few moments Connor said, "We appreciate you getting in touch about Jared. What have you got?"

"Do you know where he is?" Naomi finally asked, her voice shaky.

Pete shook his head. "No, I don't." He shifted his gaze back to Connor. "I heard about what happened and that you were looking for Jared. There's something I thought you should know, and then I want to find out what I can do to help."

"Okay, give me your information."

Normally, this would be the point where Pete would begin negotiating for payment. But this time, he didn't.

"First off, Jared's a friend of mine for years. Maybe you didn't know that."

"I did not."

"Well, he and I haven't hung out much lately because he's been getting sober and part of that involved staying away from friends like me who could drag him back into old habits. So that's the first thing I want to tell you, no matter what people might say or think, he really is serious about getting sober and staying that way. Almost makes me want to try and dry out again." Pete took a long sip of coffee. *"Almost."*

"Okay, thanks for that," Connor replied. "And you know I'll help you get set up with rehab anytime you ask."

Pete avoided eye contact with him and took another sip of coffee.

"What else?"

"I don't want to see Jared get picked up by the cops. Not after he's worked so hard to straighten his life out. And I don't for a minute think he was intentionally involved in anything bad. I'd rather he turn himself in to you. So when I heard you were trying to track him down, I looked for him but couldn't find him. I asked around and nobody's seen him since Thursday night." Pete took a sip of coffee. "I got to thinking that he's probably hiding out with a buddy. So I started contacting our mutual friends. There were three that I couldn't get hold of. I went looking at the places where they normally hang out but I couldn't find them. Eventually, they responded to my texts, but all three of them seemed kind of cagey and weird in their replies."

He reached into his pocket and pulled out a scrap of paper that looked like it had been torn off of an envelope. "These are their names and phone numbers."

He handed it to Connor, who unfolded it and glanced at the names. None of them was familiar to him. "Thanks." He refolded the paper and slid it into his pocket. "When I contact them I won't mention your name."

"I'd appreciate that."

They all got to their feet, and Naomi expressed her appreciation to Pete as they headed for the exit.

Connor opened the door and stepped out first, sweeping his gaze across their surroundings. He stepped aside for Naomi to walk out after he was certain it was safe, then he kept an eye on Pete until the informant turned a corner and disappeared from sight.

"I received a text from Tyler Copley while we were in there," Naomi said as Connor slid behind the wheel of his truck. He glanced over and she was looking at the screen of her phone. "He says he'd be happy to talk to me regarding what he learned about Stuart Furniture while doing his research before he made his offer." She glanced up. "He also seems to think my wanting to talk with him indicates that I regret my purchase and that I want to sell it to him. He's going to be disappointed to learn otherwise."

"Maybe he knows something about the furniture company that we don't know. Some detail that would point to a connection between Stuart Furniture and the attacks on you. Can he meet with us right now?"

"He says he'll be available after five o'clock."

Connor fired up the truck's engine. "Find out if he'll meet us at the Range River Bail Bonds office at five thirty."

"Okay."

They'd driven a couple of miles down the road, heading back toward the inn, when Naomi's phone chimed with Tyler's response. "He doesn't want to meet in the bail bonds office," she said. "He says he'll meet us at Rosalie's Diner over on the east end of Wolf Lake. Apparently, he likes to order food there to take home for his dinner. Says he'll sit and chat with us for a few minutes before he picks up his food and leaves."

"Works for me," Connor said.

They were nearly at the inn when Naomi's phone rang. "It's my dad."

Connor heard the note of tension that was always in her voice when she spoke of her father. "Put it on speaker."

Naomi tapped the screen. "Hello, Dad. Have you got some information about Jared?"

"What, no asking your old man how he is?"

From the corner of his eye Connor saw Naomi grimace.

"I'm really not in the mood for chitchat," she said. "I'm worried about Jared and I'm hoping you have some kind of lead."

"I do in fact have some information for you. I've seen your brother with my own eyes."

Connor pulled to the side of the road so he could focus on what Greg had to say.

"You *saw* him and *talked* to him? You know where he is?" The questions tumbled out of Naomi as excitement filled her voice. "Is he with you right now?"

"Well, now, slow down a bit."

Connor felt a sour turn in his stomach. He dealt with plenty of liars in his line of work. People who got through life dealing in half-truths and manipulations. Already this conversation did not sound good to him.

The happiness he saw on Naomi's face and the hope he heard in her voice made it even worse. He knew how it was to have an untrustworthy parent. Despite everything you knew about them, when it came to things that were critically important, you wanted to believe in them.

"I saw your brother from a distance," her dad said. "Just a few minutes ago. I'm here at Wolf Lake in the parking lot near the boat ramps. I saw him getting into a beige sedan with a couple of his friends. I yelled but they didn't hear me and they drove away before I could get to my truck and drive over to them."

"So he's still in town," Naomi said to Connor. Then she directed her attention back to her phone. "What are the names of the friends he was with?"

"That's something I can't tell you. I've just seen them with your brother a few times in the past. I don't know their names."

"Oh," Naomi said softly, sounding deflated.

"But I *do* know a friend of your brother's who might be able to tell me."

"Okay, what's that friend's name?"

"Well, now, that's complicated. I think he'd be more willing to talk to me—but even if I'm the one asking, he might need a little… incentive to open up. If you want to send me a few bucks that I can offer to the guy to get him to talk, that might get us somewhere. You know, I'm really worried about your brother. The sooner we find him, the better."

Naomi muted the call and turned to Connor. "What do you think?"

"I think it sounds suspicious."

Naomi chewed her lower lip for a few seconds. "Yeah, but what if he's telling the truth? Shouldn't we try every avenue to generate a lead?"

Connor nodded. "It's your call." If Connor had to track down a member of his family for some reason, he would try every available option. Even the long shots. He pulled the list Pete had just given him out of his pocket. "See if your dad recognizes any of these names."

Naomi unmuted the call and asked her dad about the names on the list.

"Nope," he said. "None of them sounds familiar."

"Okay," Naomi said. She sent him some money via one of her phone apps and a few moments later her dad confirmed receipt of it.

"This will help," her dad said. "I'm going to get cracking right now and I'll get you some good information. Don't worry, we're going to get your brother back home and taken care of."

After disconnecting Naomi slid the phone into her pocket and sat quietly. Just like all those years ago, in a moment of intense emotion for Naomi, Connor had no idea what to say.

"I hope your dad does find out where your brother's been staying." Connor finally forced out the words as he steered the truck back onto the road. His comment sounded pretty weak to him, but he was willing to make a fool of himself to at least try to make sure she knew that he cared.

"Thanks. I appreciate you saying that. But we both know there's a good chance my dad is just scamming me for the money," she said, sounding much less hopeful than she had a few moments ago. "Still, I suppose there is a small chance he's telling the truth."

Telling the truth, or setting you up for something. Possibly another attack.

Sometimes people genuinely wanted to help. But it was Connor's experience that sometimes when people seemed helpful they actually had ulterior motives.

As soon as they stepped inside Rosalie's Diner, Naomi spotted Tyler Copley already seated at a nearby table. He was maybe forty years old, tall and lanky, with reddish fluff for hair and rimless glasses. Naomi had spoken with him briefly when they were both touring the Stuart Furniture factory in preparation for making their bids.

"Tyler, thanks for meeting us," Naomi called out.

He looked up from his phone screen and offered a polite smile.

Several hours had passed since they'd set up the appointment to meet and during that time Naomi had been impatiently waiting to have this conversation.

Connor had spent most of the time researching the names Peter had given him and trying to call the men, but none of them had answered their phones. Naomi's dad had not responded to her texts asking for updates and further details on his sighting of Jared. Detective Romanov had not contacted Naomi or Connor with any new information, either. And so far the other bounty hunters had only been able to gather piecemeal bits of information on the two professional killers.

The lack of progress on the case had left Naomi focused on talking to Tyler and hoping for useful information.

"Please, have a seat," Tyler said after Naomi introduced Connor. "I'm sorry to hear about the harrowing experiences you've been going through. How can I help?"

"We thought that the attacks might be related to the furniture company," Naomi said. "Do you have any idea why the company would be targeted?"

He drew his brows together and frowned.

"You think all the terrible things that have happened are related to Stuart Furniture?"

"Well, somebody in the facility did throw a firebomb into the chemical storage room and lock me inside with it."

"Customers are allowed in the building," he said thoughtfully. "Plus employees, employee guests, mail carriers, even pizza delivery guys. Anybody who's been in there recently would know how lacking on-site security is."

"We've thought about that," Connor said with a slight nod. "But putting that fact aside for a moment, can you think of anyone directly connected to the factory who might hold a grudge against Naomi since she's the new owner?"

Tyler appeared to think about that for a moment. "I have heard rumors that some of the employees who stayed all the way through to the bitter end thought they'd get some kind of compensation from Mr. Berger's family in return for their loyalty when a lot of other employees were jumping ship."

"Why would they take their anger out on my brother and me?"

"I'm not saying it's reasonable. I'm just saying it's what I heard." Tyler shrugged. "And we all know that some people act irrationally and lash out when they're angry."

"What about you?" Connor asked. "Are you angry that Naomi got the business instead of you?"

Naomi's stomach tightened at the directness of the question. At the same time she leaned forward a little, curious.

Tyler's eyes widened in surprise. For a moment he just stared. Then he slowly smiled and laughed. "No, I'm not angry. I was disappointed but I got over it. I'm a self-employed accountant. I do well enough that I have a little money to invest so I've invested in several businesses in town to help the local economy. My plan was to buy the furniture factory, sell off half the property and keep part of the facility for a furniture showroom. That's all. I didn't have any big dream. I just saw an opportunity and tried to grab it. Things didn't work out, but that's life. I wasn't exactly broken up about it. I've moved on." He turned to Naomi. "Unless you've changed your plans and decided you want to sell Stuart Furniture to me."

Naomi shook her head.

"If you do change your mind let me know. I'll match the price you paid for it so you can get out of the deal without a loss."

A server walked over with a take-out bag full of food for Tyler and the three of them got to their feet. They parted ways a few moments later.

As Naomi headed toward Connor's truck, she pulled her coat collar up around her neck. It was dark out and cold, with a biting wind. On her phone app she'd been tracking the storm heading down from Alaska. It was possible it would change direction or break apart before it reached North Idaho, but if snow did fall it would stay around for a while with these frigid temperatures.

"What's your reaction to Tyler's comments?" Naomi asked as Connor started the truck and they pulled out onto the road.

"Rumors are tricky," he said. "Sometimes they're helpful and other times they send you on a wild-goose chase. Maybe it's time to talk to your manager, James, and see what he has to say about it. He should be feeling better by now. Let's see if we can talk to him tomorrow. In the meantime, I think you should stay away from the factory."

"You don't need to tell me that twice." Naomi had picked up Connor's habit of constantly scanning their surroundings. "I don't want to take any foolish risks. I think I can handle most of what needs to be done at work via email and video calls. But as soon as we get this situation solved, and the criminals arrested, I want to get back to the office."

If she came to the conclusion that she wanted to sell the furniture factory on her own for some reason, that was one thing. But being scared away by the lowlife who'd tried to burn her up, that was something else. Something she wouldn't let happen.

They drove along the winding road beside the lake. The buildings thinned out as they headed toward a stretch of forest. Several miles ahead they would approach the resort on the edge of Wolf Lake. Beyond that would be the population center and commercial heart of the town of Range River.

"Have you had a chance to call your insurance company about the damage to your house?" Connor asked.

Before Naomi could answer she heard the roar of an engine behind them and then saw white light flicker across the cab's interior. Moments later, the motorcyclist zoomed by on the driver's side, got in front of Connor's truck and abruptly slowed down, forcing Connor to slow down, as well.

"What's going on?" Naomi asked.

"I don't know. Get ready to call the cops."

More motorcyclists appeared behind them. In the darkness, Naomi could pick out the headlights of two motorcycles moving up on the driver's side, dangerously close to the truck. As they drove closer to the front of the truck, one of the motorcyclists fired a gun into the window beside Connor's head.

TEN

"Get down!" Connor leaned away from the side window as far as possible while keeping an eye on the road and the motorcyclist in front of him.

With one hand on the wheel, he reached over to touch Naomi and reassure himself that she hadn't been injured. "Are you okay?"

The motorcyclist in front of him slowed down even more. The rider who'd shot at him darted ahead and was turning around to circle back, presumably to fire again. More motorcycle headlights appeared directly behind them and Connor had too many things to keep track of to take the reassuring visual assessment of Naomi that he craved. "Were you shot?" he demanded when she didn't respond for several terrifying seconds, leaving him to imagine the worst had happened to her.

"I'm okay," she finally said in a shaky voice. "What about you?"

"Right as rain," he said tightly. The small cuts from the bits of safety glass that had blown through the window beside him stung a little but they weren't going to kill him. Further gunshots, however, just might. "Have you called 9-1-1?"

"Doing it right now."

The shooter doubled back toward them and Connor gripped the steering wheel tighter. The thought of what he was about to do made him feel a little sick, but he had no choice. "Get ready for an impact," he called out as the approaching motorcyclist lifted his gun to take aim. Connor steered directly toward him.

There was a thudding sound as the truck's fender and the front wheel of the motorcycle collided, knocking the motorcycle over and sending it sliding and scraping across the asphalt as it careened into the darkness off to the side of the road.

The rider in front of Connor slowed down even more, apparently attempting to force Connor to stop. But this time the bounty hunter hit the gas pedal and steered toward the other side of the road in an attempt to get past the guy.

The riders on his tail were pulling up closer and he would not risk getting boxed in and shot at again. Especially with Naomi beside him.

Bam!

A bullet hit the back of the truck cab right at the metal edge of the window. Now they were being targeted by the riders *behind* them.

Bam! Bam! Two more shots hit the truck just as the motorcycle ahead of them sped up and vanished in the darkness.

"Great." Connor ground out the word. "That guy's going to wait up ahead and ambush us as we drive by."

"What did you say?" Naomi asked.

He'd heard her talking for the last few seconds and knew she'd connected with an emergency operator and was explaining what was happening.

He shook his head. "Never mind."

Pondering the possibility of the shooter lying in wait ahead of them, he took his foot off the accelerator.

"The dispatcher wants to know if the motorcyclists are wearing any kind of identifying insignia," Naomi said. "Anything that might indicate that they belong to a gang."

"No." Connor had already looked for that.

His assumption had been that these were members of the Invaders motorcycle gang. But he hadn't seen any of their patches. In fact, he hadn't seen anything identifying at all.

A flicker of light in the truck's passenger side window caught his attention. The riders behind them, momentarily shaken off in the curve of the road, were now visible again. Which meant they had clear lines of sight and would probably start a new round of shooting any second now.

Connor had no choice but to accelerate even if the rider up ahead was waiting for them. He moved toward the center of the road, weaving from side to side, doing his best to circumvent any clear shots from the motorcyclist ahead or the ones behind them.

The high-pitched whine of engines had him frantically checking his mirrors again. His heart leaped into his throat when he saw the passenger side mirror fill with harsh light. The attackers were approaching on Naomi's side of the truck.

He couldn't let them take a shot at her through the window. Even hunkered down to the floorboard, where she'd wisely squeezed herself, she would still be vulnerable to a ricocheted bullet.

Or the assailant could just target Connor, causing a potentially fatal accident. Once he was taken out, Naomi would be easy prey.

Determined not to let that happen, Connor called out, "Hang on," before steering hard to the right and blocking the riders.

Bam!

The shot was followed by a sudden lurching of the truck as it dipped down at the right rear corner.

"What happened?" Naomi cried out.

"Tire's been shot." Acutely aware that they'd be sitting ducks if they stopped, Connor stomped harder on the gas pedal. But the truck, already off-balance with the blown tire, caught the edge of the pavement as they rounded through a curve in the road and they slid sideways on some loose gravel until they smacked into a thick ponderosa pine and came to a sudden stop.

"You all right?" He unfastened his seat belt while looking over at Naomi.

She stared back, wide-eyed, her glasses slightly askew. "Are we trapped?" she asked, ignoring the voice of the operator coming through her phone.

"Nah," Connor said. "But we've got to move.

Fast." The tree that had stopped their slide was at the juncture of the cab and the truck bed, so they should be able to get Naomi's door open. After a quick glance toward the road and the lights of the motorcyclists who were gathering together, probably readying to launch a final attack, he gestured toward Naomi's door. "That way."

They both slid out of the truck. Holding hands, they sprinted into the darkness.

The forest was not especially thick here. Illumination from the motorcycles began to cut through the shadows as the assailants used their headlights to search for their targets.

"We need to find cover." Connor held his gun in his free hand. He would do what he had to when it came to protecting Naomi, but getting into a firefight was not his first choice. Especially against such a large number of assailants.

Across the expanse of the forest meadow he could make out the darker line where thick forest picked up again.

Behind them, he heard the angry, impatient sounds of the bikers gunning their engines. Had some of the attackers already gotten off their motorcycles to come after them? Were they being surrounded?

There was no way to tell.

They were halfway to the tree line when the roar of engines grew louder and Connor realized the motorcycles were getting closer. Faint flashes of light appeared around and in front of them and Connor risked a backward glance to see that several of the riders had turned off the road and were pursuing them into the forest.

"Oh no," Naomi said, having apparently seen the same thing.

The tone of despair in her voice reached something deep inside him that roused a fierce determination to protect and reassure her, no matter what. "They're on street bikes," he said, wanting to give her solid, true reasons to fight back despair. "They don't have the right design or tires to go far on this terrain. We just need to keep moving."

And hope that the attackers didn't simply shine their headlights on them and shoot them like fish in a barrel.

They continued across the meadow, the gunning engines and shine of the headlights edging closer and closer.

Clutching Naomi's hand even tighter and doing his best to pull her forward even faster, they finally reached the tree line. Connor quickly moved behind her so that any person or weapon would have to go through him to get to her.

The terrain grew uneven and rocky, but they continued pressing forward into the heart of the forest. "Keep going," Connor urged, hand gripping his gun and mentally preparing himself for the moment when he might have to spin around and return fire.

Moments later, with both of them gasping for air, Naomi began to slow down. They could no longer see the illumination from motorcycle headlights or hear the rumble of the engines.

"Do you think we shook them off?" Naomi asked between gasps as the ground began to slope upward.

"Maybe." *Maybe not.*

She slowed even more and her steps became fumbling, probably from fatigue and disorientation—it was especially challenging to keep pressing forward when they couldn't see clearly where they were going. Finally, she stopped. "I need to rest for a minute."

Maybe they should just stay here until the police arrived and found the truck over by the side of the road. Connor hesitated to reach for his phone, or ask Naomi to use hers. Assuming she hadn't dropped it somewhere along the way in their wild run. They'd worked too hard to elude their pursuers to do something foolish like light up the darkness with their phones or risk any sound that would draw attention to them.

They remained still for several moments.

The forest was quiet. At first, the only thing Connor could hear was the rasping sound of his own breaths along with Naomi's as they tried to recover from their sprint. Then he heard the whispering sound of the cold breeze stirring the branches overhead.

Snick.

What was that? Connor cut his gaze to the right, the direction the sound had come from, hoping that it was just the sound of the wind. Or maybe a woodland creature knocking something over.

Snick. It was a small sound. And this time he realized it sounded metallic.

Fear flared through his chest as he pictured a gun readied and aimed at Naomi. He gripped her arm to help her to her feet. "What?" she asked, seeming not to have heard anything.

Nearby, an engine roared to life followed by the sudden illumination of a headlight.

Bang!

At least one rider had managed to push their motorcycle through the forest before turning on the light to pinpoint Connor and Naomi and firing at them. Was it just one biker or were there more?

By now Connor had Naomi on her feet and moving. *"Run!"*

Easier said than done.

They ran between the trees to the sound of three more shots being fired in their direction. They made some headway, getting into the shadows beyond the beam of the headlight. Connor had hoped that they'd escaped, only to hear the whine of the engine as the motorcyclist pursued them deeper into the forest.

"I thought you said these motorcycles couldn't go far on rugged terrain," Naomi said, through deep gasps.

"They can't." He glanced around, realized they were near the base of a rocky hillside cliff and grabbed Naomi's hand to pull her alongside him toward it. He gave her a boost and she began climbing. He started up right behind her, digging into whatever fingerhold or tochold he could find in the fissured rock.

The motorcyclist roared up to a spot below them until he couldn't go any farther. Before the pursuer could start firing again, Connor urged Naomi around a curve in the cliff's face that would take them out of the shooter's line of sight.

They were partially hidden when the engine suddenly silenced.

Connor could only imagine that the shooter had gotten off the motorcycle and was coming after them on foot. He clambered up more quickly, taking care to continue partially shielding Naomi's body with his own. As they continued to climb, he listened for the sounds of someone coming up behind them.

Instead, he heard the faint wail of a siren. "Finally." *Thank You, Lord.*

"The police," Naomi said wearily.

"Yes."

They reached the top of the cliff, where Connor wrapped one arm around Naomi while keeping his gun at the ready and an eye out for their pursuer.

"Go ahead and call 9-1-1 so we can tell dispatcher where we are and that there may still be gunmen here."

His words were barely out before he heard the sound of motorcycles retreating.

Nevertheless, he remained vigilant while

Naomi spoke into her phone in a low voice, giving updated information to the dispatcher. He tightened his hold on her, his heart still pounding in his chest with fear at how close he'd come to losing her to a vicious attacker. But even as his pulse slowed and he started to calm, he knew the danger wasn't over. It was just put off for a little while longer.

Naomi leaned against the side of a patrol car with a blanket wrapped around her shoulders. The temperature was dropping fast but she didn't want to wait inside the vehicle and miss out on the conversation between Detective Romanov and Connor as Connor's damaged pickup was loaded onto the back of a flatbed tow truck. Officers were searching the road as well as the path Connor and Naomi had taken into the woods, looking for clues or physical evidence that might have been left behind in the attack.

"There's no criminal record showing up for Tyler Copley," an officer walked up and reported to Romanov.

Connor had told the detective that he and Naomi had met with the businessman just before the attempt on their lives. He'd thought there could be a connection between the two events—that maybe Tyler had told the motor-cycle gang where and when to find them—but maybe not.

"We're sure the Invaders were involved," Naomi said. "It just makes sense." It was the first thing she and Connor had talked about once the terror of the pursuit subsided. On the cliffside, they'd sat together for a moment, his arm wrapped around her, the even pulse of his heart a reassuring sound as she pressed the side of her head against his chest. In that moment she'd once again been reminded of how steady Connor had always been. He might not have al-ways known how to talk through a tough situ-ation—especially an emotional one—but he'd never actually run away from one.

She had been the one who had done that. She was the one who had pushed him away and then left town, dealing with her heartbreak over the loss of their unborn baby by blaming him for not making her feel better.

Now, gazing at him as he stood in front of her in the flicker of red and blue lights, she wanted to extend him another apology. A stronger one. That desire was prompted partly by the sincere regret about how she'd treated him. She had learned a lot about life and herself in the two decades they'd been apart, and spending time with him after so many years had brought those realizations to the forefront of her mind. Beyond that, she could no longer deny—to herself, at least—that her fears and hesitations about letting her emotional guard down around him had melted away.

The detective turned to Naomi. "I agree that the Invaders are the most obvious suspects. But Connor confirmed that the attackers weren't wearing any kind of patches or gang insignia, and that is surprising to me."

"Why? Wouldn't wearing all that stuff be akin to wearing a name tag while committing a crime?"

"Yes. And that's precisely why I'm surprised. A member of an outlaw gang has made a choice and they aren't going to shy away from it. The whole idea of being in a gang is to make your name notorious so other gangs or criminals fear you. Reputation is everything. There's no value to them in being subtle."

"But maybe this time was different for some reason."

Romanov shrugged. "It's possible. Another option is that this could have been a rival gang, looking to get in on the action. The Invaders have pumped up their game the last three or four years and gotten a solid network established for drug distribution, car theft and chop shops where they resell the car or motorcycle parts, burglaries, strong-arm robbery, extortion, all kinds of things."

"Then why are they still on the streets?" Naomi asked. "Why haven't you locked them all up?"

"We arrest the ones we can. But a lot of the criminals who are tasked to commit the most blatant crimes are lower-ranking members of the gang. Arresting them doesn't stop anything—there are always plenty of guys rising through the ranks who are eager to take their place. Meanwhile, the gang leaders have established a sophisticated organization. *They* are the ones we need to capture to stop everything, but they don't get their hands dirty. We're always trying to build a case against them, but it isn't easy." She cut a glance at Connor. "And while we put forth that effort, we need everyone else to stay away from them."

Connor nodded. "Yes, ma'am."

"Did you see anyone who looked familiar among the bikers?" Romanov asked. "Kevin

Ashton's murderers, Almada and Olsen, are known to work with organized crime. That would include criminal motorcycle gangs."

Naomi shook her head. "I wasn't able to see anyone's face. It was too dark, and they were wearing helmets, anyway."

"Same here," Connor added. "I didn't see anyone's face, either."

"Does Jared have a motorcycle?" Romanov asked. "Is he into biker culture?"

"Not that I've ever seen, and he's never mentioned it. Why? Do you think he's an Invader?" Naomi rolled her eyes at the absurdity of the idea and then shook her head. "That's not like him at all."

"Perhaps your bother made someone in the Invaders angry," the detective said. "Or somehow he crossed one of their rival gangs." She paused for a moment and then shook her head slightly. "But I don't see how that would lead to someone targeting you with such determination."

"Believe me, I've been trying to mentally retrace everything I've done since I've moved back to town, hoping I'd think of something that might have triggered someone," Naomi replied. "But I can't think of anything."

"What about your father? Have you ever known him to have any kind of interaction with the Invaders or any other group like them?"

Naomi let out a heavy sigh. "I haven't been keeping up with him over the years. I suppose when it comes to criminal alliances, anything's possible. But I don't believe he'd hurt my brother. In fact, he's helping Connor and me search for Jared. He said he saw my brother with a couple of other people but he wasn't able to catch up with him to talk to him. Now my dad's trying to figure out exactly who Jared was with. Maybe they're people who know where he is right now."

"And you didn't tell me about this lead?" Romanov arched an eyebrow and turned to Connor.

"I didn't exactly consider it a lead," Connor said. "Not without more information or proof that it actually was Naomi's brother—and that the people he was with can be identified."

"Where's this location where Jared was reportedly spotted?"

"In the parking lot near the boat docks on this side of Wolf Lake."

"All right. Let me see if I can get any exterior security video footage of the area. Maybe that will tell us something. Right now we're stretched pretty thin investigating Kevin Ashton's murder." She glanced at Connor. "If we can get any actionable information from the video footage I'll make sure that gets to you for follow-up. Any extra help right now would be appreciated."

"You've got it," Connor said.

The police were wrapping things up when Wade and Danny arrived to give Connor and Naomi a ride back to the inn.

The detective's gaze flickered in their direction before she settled it back on Naomi. "The longer Jared stays in hiding, the worse it looks for him."

"I don't know where he is," Naomi protested. "I'm not hiding him."

"I'd suggest you find him as soon as possible. Your brother has criminal connections," Romanov said, turning to walk back to her unmarked police car. "And your father has criminal connections, as well. That kind of lifestyle makes for dangerous enemies. People willing to attack a rival's family for their own nefarious reasons. Your future looks very bleak if we don't get this wrapped up quickly."

ELEVEN

"It's obvious now that the Invaders are somehow involved in all of this," Wade said as he sat down on the edge of his desk the day after the motorcycle swarm attack.

"Certainly looks that way," Connor agreed, "but Detective Romanov doesn't want us doing any investigative work that would put us in direct contact with the motorcycle gang and we're going to respect her wishes."

Connor had called a meeting at the office in the early afternoon. Right now, Wade, Danny, Hayley and her husband, Jack, were seated in front of him. Jack had arranged for the top employees at his own bail bonds business to take care of things as much as possible while he helped his wife's family.

Connor glanced at Naomi, who was also at the meeting, seated in a desk chair and paying close attention. She'd been quiet since last night's murder attempt, understandably unnerved by it. At the moment Connor was heavily focused on finding Jared since recovering him seemed to be the one thing that could convince Naomi to go into hiding at the inn until the bad guys were caught.

"Give me a summary on where you're at with your search for Almada and Olsen," Connor said to his team. He was very close to pulling them off of that manhunt and redirecting them to help with finding Naomi's brother.

"So the police are of course actively looking for them for their open murder investigation," Danny responded, leaning back in his chair and crossing his booted feet at the ankles. "Which means lots of our usual informants are afraid to talk to us. The case is just too hot right now. We've checked out the few leads we were given, but they didn't turn into anything significant." He sighed heavily. "At this point none of us has a gut feeling on where they might be. They could have left town. They could still be in town, but since they're professionals they would know how to stay out of sight."

"Having the Invaders involved in all of this would also explain why people are too afraid to talk to us," Hayley added. She shrugged. "I can't say I blame them."

"So what's next?" Naomi asked sullenly. "Is there nothing else we can do to find Jared before Almada and Olsen do?" She looked down at her hands on the desk in front of her. "Or before they succeed in killing me?" she asked quietly.

"We are *not* going to give up," Hayley said forcefully. "But we may need to take a step back on the physical search for the moment since it's not getting us anywhere. Instead, we can focus on online research and some phone calls." The bounty hunter reached up to tuck her reddish blond hair behind her ears. "We might be able to generate leads from Almada and Olsen's original bail agent or from other bounty hunters who have searched for them. We could track down former landlords or maybe employers if they've had a legitimate employment history and see if we can get background information on them that will help narrow down where they might go or who they might contact. Maybe the name of a friend or even find a particular chain restaurant they usually frequent. Something like that. People are generally creatures of habit. We try to use whatever we can from their past to predict what they might be doing right now."

"Sounds like a good plan," Connor said. "While you guys are here at the office working on that, I've got a possible lead to follow up on."

"You do?" Naomi pushed her glasses a little closer to her eyes. The practical black frames had held up well despite the assaults she'd been through.

Connor nodded. "You remember the three names Pete Slack gave us when we met at the sandwich shop? The mutual friends he had with Jared that he hadn't been able to contact lately and that he thought could possibly be helping to hide him?"

Naomi nodded.

"Earlier today, while you were resting in your room at the inn, I managed to get hold of two of them. I called, left messages telling them the truth of why I was calling, and they actually called me back. Each of them said that they didn't know where Jared was and both of them made a point of telling me that they believed he had genuinely sobered up and straightened out."

"Maybe something from his past has prompted all of this," Wade suggested.

"Or maybe it's connected to something from your dad's past," Danny said with an apologetic look at Naomi. "I'm sorry to bring that up, but I feel like it's the elephant in the room that we need to take a closer look at."

"I agree it could have something to do with my dad's criminal past," Naomi replied. "But I can't imagine that it's something my dad is actively involved in right now." She pursed her lips together for a moment. "And if it is connected to him, I don't think it's a situation he knows anything about. He would have said something if he did. He would have helped us find Jared and helped the police find Kevin's killers if he could."

Her words had sped up as she finished expressing her thought, with an emphasis that made Connor think she was trying to convince herself instead of them. Connor's heart ached in sympathy. Having grown up in a violent, tumultuous alcoholic family himself, he knew what it was like to want to trust your parents. To want to believe that they always had their children's best interests at heart.

He also knew what it was like to be bitterly disappointed but still to irrationally keep hoping that *this* time they would come through.

Naomi's dad was still ignoring her text requests for updates. There wasn't much more they could do. Investigating the man's current criminal behavior—if in fact there was any—was clearly up to Detective Romanov and the Range River PD. And Connor had no doubt the highly capable detective was already looking into that.

"Pete has agreed to meet me and take me to the place where the guy who won't return my calls—his name is Robby—works. Maybe Robby is giving your brother a place to hide out. Or maybe he's not actively involved but knows Jared's whereabouts." Connor had a pen in his hand and he tapped it on the desk. "Like any other potential lead it could turn out to be nothing, but it's worth a try."

Naomi got to her feet. "I'll go with you."

Nervous tension instantly coiled in the pit of Connor's stomach. He wanted to keep Naomi safe and doing that would depend—at least in part—on her agreeing to what he was about to say. And he was more than a little afraid that she would not. "I was hoping you wouldn't come along. I know you believe being visible in the search for your brother will encourage him to surrender to you. But even if that's true, now we're at a point where it's too dangerous for you to be out in public so visibly."

Naomi tilted her head slightly, appearing to consider his words. "I understand what you're saying. And believe me, I realize that being with me puts you in the crosshairs of any potential assassin."

Connor shook his head. "My safety is not what I'm concerned about."

Naomi smiled softly, and a little bit sadly, in return. "I know you're not concerned about yourself. And I want to thank you, all of you, for putting yourselves at risk working on my case." She looked around the room at each of the bounty hunters. Then she turned back to Connor. "Since this person, Robby, is an actual *friend* of Jared's and not simply a random informant who may know something, I'd still like to go along. Even if he doesn't know where my brother is, maybe he can give me some small scrap of personal information about Jared. Something about him that I don't already know. Despite staying in contact by phone or messaging over the years, I missed out on learning some of the small details of who Jared actually is. And I'd like to learn some of those if I can." She cleared her throat. "Especially since there's a possibility that he could be killed before I get to see him again."

"All right," Connor said. He still didn't like

the idea of exposing her to yet another possible attack, but after what she'd just said about her brother, how could he argue?

Range River Bail Bonds owned multiple vehicles, so Connor had an SUV he could use while his truck was being repaired. Pete had agreed to meet Connor and Naomi at Carpet Corral, where Robby worked. Connor had asked him not to tell Robby they were coming. Catching the potential informant off guard without the opportunity to prepare any lies in advance could possibly result in more truthful answers.

As Connor drove to Carpet Corral, a sprinkling of icy rain splattered across the windshield. Beside him, Naomi pulled out her phone. "They're predicting scattered moderate snow showers for tonight," she said, looking at the screen. "The heavier snowfall is supposed to start coming down tomorrow night and it will settle in for a couple of days. Looks like it's going to be a pretty good accumulation."

"The dogs will be happy," Connor said, looking around at the vehicles beside and ahead of them and then checking the rearview mirror. "They love getting out and playing in the snow after a storm clears."

Connor was on edge, but he was trying to appear calm for Naomi's sake. He felt a little more secure in a less recognizable vehicle. Perhaps the attackers wouldn't realize it was them. He would hope that was the case but he couldn't count on it.

He glanced over at Naomi. Her dark hair and eyes had always appealed to him. And there was something about her face that, even viewed in profile, made her look kind and compassionate yet also strong and determined. Maybe it was the stubborn set of her jawline combined with the soft line of her lips. Or maybe it was the way she drew together her dark brows when she was thinking deeply. Like she was doing right now.

It felt so right to be here riding alongside her. There had been moments over the last three days when it felt as if their years apart had never happened. Admittedly the circumstances that had brought them together—and kept them together—were horrible. And yet, well, here they were. Together again. Despite his earlier determination to keep his distance emotionally, now he couldn't help wondering—and hoping—that Naomi was feeling something similar.

Suddenly realizing the direction his thoughts

were going, he quickly reined them in. Naomi's life was in danger and keeping her safe was what he needed to stay focused on. Maybe later, if they both survived, he would find out how she felt about him and whether she thought there was any chance for them.

"I'm going to call my dad," Naomi said as they continued along the winding road. "See if he's learned anything about the people he saw with Jared." She glanced at Connor. "Or if Detective Romanov has gone by his house to question him about his own activities."

"Okay," Connor said evenly.

She put the phone on speaker, tapped the screen, and after several rings it went to voice mail. "Hey, Dad, it's me. Call me as soon as you get a chance. Please."

Her voice sounded small and uncertain to Connor. As if she were a kid again.

Connor felt sad for her, but he had no clue what to say to make her feel better. That was just not a skill he naturally had.

"I know your dad has disappointed you in the past," he said, finally deciding to take a chance on just giving voice to what he honestly thought and felt. "I don't know if he's changed much over the years. But you have me. And my family. We care about you and you can lean on us anytime you want to. We won't let you down."

Naomi began to sniff. She cleared her throat a few times and then she began crying quietly.

Connor was flooded with panic. *What have I done?*

"Thank you," Naomi eventually said after composing herself. "I appreciate that. Truly, it means a lot to me."

Really? He'd actually managed to say the right thing?

"Of course," he replied, figuring it would be wise to keep his response to a minimum before he ruined the moment.

They drove a little longer until they reached a section of town with retail stores and shopper-friendly warehouses. Connor spotted the barn-shaped outline of Carpet Corral as he drove closer. Pete was standing in the parking lot.

Connor pulled into a slot far away from any other vehicles. After taking a few moments to look around to make sure the situation was safe, he and Naomi got out of the SUV.

"Hey," Pete called in greeting as he walked up to them. "Robby should be coming out soon for his afternoon break. He usually sits in his car to have some privacy if he wants to talk on his phone or just to get away from his co-workers for a bit."

A short time later a heavyset young man with a dark beard walked out a side door.

"That's him." Pete headed toward Robby with Connor and Naomi following. "Robby, this is Jared's sister, Naomi, and a friend of hers. They want to talk to you for a minute."

Robby didn't look especially thrilled, but he wasn't upset enough to push past them on the way to his sedan. He stopped and looked at them while Pete kept up a stream of friendly banter that Connor figured was meant to help keep Robby calm.

"I was sorry to hear about the stuff that happened to Jared," Robby said after a moment's hesitation, his attention focused on Naomi. "I was especially sad to hear that Kevin was murdered. He was a good guy. Helped me a lot. Helped tons of people and he didn't deserve what happened to him."

"That's why I'm so anxious to find my brother," Naomi said. "The same men who killed Kevin tried to kill Jared and me, too. And they haven't stopped trying. I was nearly killed just last night. I'm afraid they're after Jared, too."

"People have tried to kill you?"

She nodded and described the explosion at her home, the fire at her furniture company, and last night's motorcycle-swarm attempted shooting of her and Connor.

"Where is Jared?" Connor took a chance on asking directly after seeing the expression of concern on Robby's face.

Robby shook his head. "I don't know. I haven't seen him. But if I do, I'll let him know his sister is looking for him." He glanced at his phone. "I should get back to work."

Before he could walk away Connor asked, "Who do you know that drives a beige sedan and might have been with Jared by the boat docks yesterday?" Maybe he could help turn Naomi's father's report of the sighting into a workable lead.

Robby shrugged. "No one."

Connor waited until he'd walked inside the carpet store and shut the door behind him before turning to Pete and asking, "What do you think? You know him. Do you believe he's being forthright or is he hiding something?"

"It's hard to say." Pete shook his head slightly. "Bringing you two to talk to him without warning made him tense. Understandably."

"If he talks to you about this later, let us know."

"I will."

"What about the beige sedan and the friends supposedly with Jared by the boat docks that you just heard me mention to Robby? Does any of that sound familiar?"

Pete shook his head. "No. But I'll keep asking around and trying to get the word out that Jared needs to turn himself in."

Icy rain, like the brief smattering that had passed by a short while ago, began to fall again. This time, though, it didn't seem like it would be moving on very quickly. Pete flipped up his jacket collar. "Sorry this meeting didn't give you answers, but I'll keep doing what I can." With that, he walked quickly toward a small, battered pickup truck.

Connor and Naomi headed back to the SUV. On a nearby street, Connor heard the sound of a motorcyclist gunning the engine. Heart speeding up in his chest in anticipation of another attack, he rested a hand on his hip near his gun as he urged Naomi to move faster.

Once they were inside the SUV he waited several moments, watching Pete drive away and also watching the road. Meanwhile, the sound of the motorcycle faded away. As he finally started driving, he looked for signs of a trap or an ambush. He didn't necessarily trust

Pete or Robby. It was possible this meeting was a setup of some sort. But getting out and taking risks was part of his job. He glanced over at Naomi, who was wiping rainwater off of her eyeglasses with the hem of her shirt. Perhaps it was selfish of him, but he was grateful that she had accompanied him to this meeting. He appreciated any chance to spend more time with her.

"Well, that was disappointing," she said after a few moments. "I was hoping Robby would know something useful. The longer this goes on, the more worried I am about Jared."

"I understand," Connor said. "But right now I'm more worried about you."

He continued to stay alert to their surroundings as his thoughts shifted to the Riverside Inn. Normally, it was a refuge and safe place for the entire bounty hunting crew whenever they needed it. He'd housed people who were in danger there in the past and no one had ever dared attempt a direct assault on his home. But the situation now, with Naomi, felt much more threatening and dire than any investigation he'd been involved with in the past. It was as if the person or persons behind the attacks— whoever it was who had hired Almada and Olsen—had lost their sense of reason. They were taking irrational risks, like the attack on a public highway last night, to get to Naomi.

Connor considered that he might be over-reacting. Perhaps it wasn't the attacks themselves that had him worried so much as the fact that they were directed at someone he cared about so much. Maybe even loved. Possibly had never stopped loving.

He pressed the accelerator a little harder, anxious to get back to the inn. He wanted to check and recheck the locks and alarms and everything he could think of. He wanted to make sure Naomi was safe. Then he wanted to go looking for her brother. Maybe along the way he would learn something that could help put a stop to these vicious criminal actions.

TWELVE

Jared might not even still be alive.

The thought crossed Naomi's mind, triggering a shuddering chill that passed through her body.

What if something horrible had happened to her younger brother and she hadn't been there to help him? Like she hadn't been around to run interference between him and their parents after she married Connor and moved out as a teenager.

And what if there was another attack and she was killed? The prospect of that felt frighteningly possible. A second chill raced through her bloodstream and she wrapped her arms around her body hoping the warmth from that, along with the heat from the fireplace in front of her, would help her feel more secure.

It didn't work.

In the aftermath of the disappointing meeting with Robby a couple of hours ago, dark emotions had settled over her that were much heavier than she had anticipated. It wasn't because of the meeting, really. It was just that the meeting was one more thing on top of the pile that hadn't gone the way she'd wanted. The terrifying and tumultuous feelings of the last three days were finally starting to catch up with her.

She was tired. Physically and emotionally. And mentally, she'd come to a dead stop when she'd tried to think of new ideas or ways to find Jared.

One of the burning logs in the fireplace made a cracking and popping noise, sending a thin column of sparks drifting up the chimney. For the moment she was alone with her thoughts in the great room at the inn. Connor was in his office while Wade and Charlotte were in the kitchen helping Maribel with dinner. There'd been no specific task available for Naomi to help them, so she'd decided to get out of the way and sit in the great room, where she could take a few moments alone to process the emotions that were spinning inside of her.

That might have been a mistake.

Because beyond her feelings about her

brother and what his circumstances were at this moment, she was also processing her feelings for Connor. And she couldn't deny that there was truly something there. Something beyond her appreciation of the man's heroic efforts to protect her and keep her safe and help her find Jared. Something about Connor personally—his compassion and sense of humor and generosity of spirit, especially when it came to helping people. *Or animals*, she thought, glancing at a pair of skinny old cats sleeping side by side on a thickly cushioned chair.

The thing was, could she really trust those feelings? Could she trust her judgment when it came to something like this? She blamed herself and her judgment—or lack thereof, really—for the end of their marriage.

She wanted to believe that her judgment had gotten better since then. She'd had many years of wonderful marriage with her second husband, and after becoming a Christian and marrying Matt, Naomi had become more stable and clear-thinking. Or had she? Maybe the calm attitude and sensible decision-making she associated with herself had all been due to the influence and presence of Matt in her life. What if her feelings toward Connor right now were due to the drama of the situation she was in? What if acting on them would be the second biggest mistake of her life?

She didn't want to get hurt again. And she definitely didn't want to end up hurting Connor again, either.

When it came to business decisions, she was solid. But when it came to something like her strong attraction to her former husband, she wasn't so sure.

An electronic chime sounded from the direction of the home office where Connor was working. Immediately the door flew open and Connor headed in Naomi's direction, phone in hand.

Naomi sat up ramrod straight, fear like an electric current running up her spine. "What's wrong?" she called out loudly enough to wake the sleeping cats.

"Someone's crossed the security perimeter. They're approaching the inn."

Naomi told herself it could just be some poor soul whose car broke down nearby who was looking for help. Still, her heart was already racing and her gaze darted toward the glass sliding door and any other areas where an attacker could gain entrance. Or simply start shooting.

"Are you seeing this?" Wade asked, walking into the great room with his phone in his hand. Maribel and Charlotte followed him.

"Yep." Connor already had the smart screen at one end of the room turned on and he synced the image from his phone onto it.

Several images of the exterior of the inn appeared and Connor enlarged one. "I see movement here," he said to Wade. "You keep an eye on the other angles on your phone. Could be more than one person."

Charlotte and Maribel quickly moved to make certain all the doors and windows were secure.

Meanwhile, Naomi kept her gaze focused on the screen. It was dark outside and a light snow was falling. A man, with the hood of his jacket pulled up over his head, hiding much of his face, walked through the pine trees toward the main entrance of the inn. The image was fuzzy and in shades of gray instead of color.

"Infrared?" Naomi asked quietly, staring at the image while wondering how many other people might be closing in on them.

"Yes. We'll stay with that so we don't scare him away before we can capture better pictures of him. After he gets closer we'll turn on the floodlights. If he's just a normal person whose car broke down nearby then having the light come on shouldn't scare him away."

"I'm not seeing anybody else," Wade said, eyes glued to his phone. "Just the one guy."

"He's got his hands in his pockets so I don't know if he's got a weapon," Connor commented.

The figure moved closer and Naomi began feeling like there was something familiar about him. But she wasn't sure what it was that had caught her eye. "Do you think you've seen this man before?" she asked Connor.

"No. Do you?"

There was something about the set of the man's shoulders. Or maybe it was the way he walked. Then he looked up at a camera.

"Jared."

Naomi jumped up and hurried to open the front door.

Connor blocked her way. "Let's slow down."

Wade had already caught up with them in the foyer and Naomi couldn't miss seeing that both men had guns in their hands.

"You're not going to shoot my brother," she said, panic starting to claw its way up her throat.

"We don't know who else might be nearby hiding out of sight," Connor responded, his voice tight with tension. "He could be showing up here under duress. Someone might have a weapon aimed at him, forcing him to try to get you to open the door."

Naomi fought to draw a breath into her tight lungs.

"Step back," Connor said.

She moved aside and Connor and Wade moved up to the door. After nodding to one another, indicating they were both ready, Connor slowly opened it. Wade tapped his phone and light flooded the front of the building.

Jared startled before looking toward the door with slightly squinted eyes.

Naomi had already moved so that she could see between Connor and Wade.

Her heart broke at the sight of her brother, appearing thin and pale and shivering in the falling snow. "Jared! Are you okay?"

Connor again moved so that she could not squeeze past him. "You alone?" he called out to Jared.

"Yeah. I had someone drop me at the roadside and I walked the rest of the way here."

"Who dropped you off?"

"Look, I don't want him to get charged with aiding a fugitive so I'm not going to say."

Connor stepped forward onto the porch and

frisked Jared before finally letting him into the house.

Naomi grabbed her brother in a bear hug, not caring that he was damp from the snow. "I'm so grateful you're alive!"

"You, too, sis," he said, returning the embrace.

"Where have you been?" Naomi demanded. "Why did you take off and hide?"

"A friend let me stay at his family's fishing cabin." He sighed heavily. "I took off because I was afraid of getting locked up." He glanced at Connor with a sheepish expression. "I knew the cops would assume I'd intentionally killed Kevin, at least at first, and I just couldn't stand that. I thought that maybe after a few days of investigation they'd have time to examine evidence at the murder scene and take into consideration that I might have been framed." Now he was looking at Naomi again. "And at that point maybe they wouldn't be so quick to believe the worst of me."

"So why are you here now?" Connor asked.

Again, Jared focused on his sister. "I honestly thought you'd be okay. I never dreamed whoever is behind all of this would keep attacking you. When I learned about that I knew it was time for me to turn myself in. I'm so sorry. I feel responsible even though I didn't do anything wrong. I didn't murder Kevin and I didn't do anything that led to him being murdered."

"What were you doing in town with the two men and the beige sedan?" Naomi asked. "Who were they?"

"Huh?" Jared's expression went blank.

"Near the boat docks?" she prompted. "Dad said he saw you there."

"No, he didn't. Whoever he saw, it wasn't me. I was at the fishing cabin from a couple hours after the last time I saw you guys until now."

Naomi felt a little sick. Her dad had *lied* to her. When he'd said he saw her brother, he'd made up the whole thing. She assumed it was for the money.

She exchanged glances with Connor and thought she saw an expression of pity on his face. That made her feel even worse. He probably felt sorry for her because he knew how badly she'd wanted to believe in her dad. It was looking like her earlier concern was something to consider more closely. Maybe she'd been right to question whether her judgment had actually improved. Maybe it had been Matt's wisdom over the years of their married life that had made her feel like she'd gained discernment that she didn't really have at all.

Maybe, among other things, she needed to extinguish her attraction to Connor before things between them went any further.

Connor cleared his throat. "Jared, you know I have to take you to the police station right now."

"Yes."

"I'll call Detective Romanov and tell her we have Jared in custody," Wade said quietly before walking farther into the great room, tapping his phone screen and putting it up to his ear.

By now Maribel and Charlotte were standing by watching. Connor gave Maribel a nod and she went into his office. She came back out a moment later with Connor's handcuffs and handed them to him.

"I've got to do this since you bailed on me before," Connor said, collecting Jared's hands behind his back and cuffing them.

"Sorry," Jared said sadly to his sister. "Guess I'll see you later."

"Oh no." Naomi shook her head emphatically. "I'm going with you to the police station. And I'll be calling my own lawyer to get a referral on an excellent criminal defense lawyer on the way there. I'm not giving up on you."

"Thanks," Jared said softly, tears starting to roll down his cheeks.

"Get your truck and drive into town behind us," Connor called over to Wade. "This would be the perfect time for the criminals to launch another attack."

Naomi felt the blood leave her face at the thought of someone coming after her yet again—and when she had Jared with her, too. At the beginning the attackers had attempted to kill *both* Naomi and Jared. Finding them together, which was the situation now, would be exactly what they wanted.

"Disappearing like you did was a stupid stunt." Detective Romanov sat back in her desk chair and crossed her arms over her chest.

Connor, leaning in the doorway of Romanov's office at the police station, watched as Jared, head lowered, nodded and said, "Yes, ma'am. I understand that and I'm sorry."

Naomi sat in the visitor's chair beside her brother, her face tight with tension.

The feeling of relief Connor had hoped she would feel with the recovery of her brother had obviously not happened. The entire ride over she'd been on the phone with her attorney, getting some general advice while waiting to hear back from a criminal attorney her lawyer had recommended. Her fear for her brother's future had come through loud and clear.

And then there was the fear she must be feeling for herself. After all, whoever had launched the attacks targeting Naomi was still at large. Jared surrendering himself to the authorities didn't change that. Naomi was still in danger.

"You're going to have to go before a magistrate to determine if you're eligible for a new bond," the detective added. "Given that you're an obvious flight risk, I wouldn't count on it."

"Will you be charging him with Kevin Ashton's murder?" Connor asked.

Jared lifted his head. Both he and his sister locked their gazes on the detective.

"It's quite possible."

That's not a yes.

"I want to know everything about whoever has been hiding you all this time," Romanov prodded.

She wants to make it appear that in return for information she will drop any potential murder charges. Her response told Connor that for the moment she didn't have any evidence that would justify charging Jared with the murder. That was good news. But there were still the original drug-trafficking charges that had been leveled against him. Obviously, the previous plea deal in that situation would have to be renegotiated after all that had happened. And there was the problem of him having missed his court appointment and officially becoming a fugitive. Romanov had plenty to work with if she wanted to play hardball.

"I don't want the friend who helped me to get into trouble."

Romanov shrugged. "You're going to be locked up overnight no matter what. Why don't you think about it while you're waiting to see the magistrate in the morning?"

Jared cleared his throat while trying to hold back a sob. He'd made it abundantly clear he really didn't want to go to jail. That he feared for his life there.

"What are you going to do to ensure his safety tonight?" Naomi demanded, a hint of steel to her voice.

She was upset but she was not going to let herself fall apart. Connor could see the determination in her eyes and in the rest of her body as she sat up straighter and squared her shoulders.

"Given all the attacks over the last three days, I can assure you that I'm focused on your brother's safety as well as *your* safety. We'll be housing him separately from any other prisoners."

The detective gestured at someone through the glass between her office and the squad room. Connor turned and then stepped aside to make room for two officers who had come to collect Jared and take him to lockup. The siblings were not allowed to embrace before they said goodbye.

Connor walked toward the interior of Romanov's office and took the chair Jared had just vacated. He reached for Naomi's hand and squeezed it. She didn't squeeze back. Instead, she pulled her hand away from his to tuck her hair behind her ear.

"What can I do to help my brother?" Naomi asked Romanov.

"You've done the best thing for him by bringing him here."

"Can you give us any updates on your investigation?" Connor asked.

The detective held his gaze for a long, uncomfortable moment, making it painfully clear that she was not obligated to tell him anything. "You do realize this is my investigation and not yours?" she finally said.

"Yes, ma'am."

She nodded, seemingly satisfied with that. "We located the murder weapon. Through ballistics testing, we were able to connect it to a prior murder involving one of the attackers the two of you identified. We're also getting some helpful results in looking at security video from neighboring houses on Kevin Ashton's street as well as businesses on the waterfront across the river."

Naomi blew out a small sigh of relief. "So, you'll be able to see—and prove—that the statement I gave you about what happened is true."

"The investigation is ongoing," Romanov said neutrally.

"Do you have any new information on Olsen and Almada?" Connor asked, again risking the detective's ire. "Or the Invaders?" He would risk his working relationship with Romanov if he had to. Anything it took to keep Naomi safe. He needed to know where to anticipate attacks from if that were at all possible. Hopefully, the detective would be only mildly annoyed with his persistent questioning.

Romanov leveled her gaze at him, but she didn't appear particularly annoyed. "I have no comment on that other than to suggest that you continue to stay at the Riverside Inn for the time being." By now her attention was turned toward Naomi and the last part of the statement was obviously directed at her. "I want to make certain that you do not think you are safer with your brother in custody. Because you aren't. Frankly, I would expect the attacks to intensify now. I would assume they've been looking for Jared all this time. Now, since he's in police custody, they'll be able to focus all their attention on you. You might want to keep a low profile around town for the time being."

"Okay," Naomi said quietly.

With that, the detective stood and it was clear their meeting was over. "Watch your backs," Romanov said as they left her office.

On their way out, Connor tried to walk beside Naomi in the hallway but she seemed determined to not match her stride with his and to stay too far away for him to take her hand.

Maybe she was upset about her brother. Maybe this had nothing to do with Connor. Or maybe he'd been mistaken to think that there'd been a growing connection between them.

He wouldn't push her. Absolutely not. Never. If she wanted some distance that was fine. No problem. But he hoped it was only a temporary situation.

Perhaps she just needed some time to process what was going on with her and her brother.

"I'll need to go back to my house tonight or tomorrow and get some more clothes since there's no telling how long I'll be staying at the inn," Naomi said as they reached the exit.

Ah, so that was it. Her thoughts had been focused on planning ahead. Good for her.

"And I don't know when I'll be able to have the repairs completed on the damage done by the explosion. I still need to have someone from the insurance company come out and take a look at it. Then I'll need to get estimates from contractors." She shook her head. "I guess the best thing to do is make sure the temporary repairs will hold up through winter."

"I can help with that." Connor pulled open the door and gestured for her to hold back for a moment while he walked past her and scanned the street and the area around the building. Even though it was the police department, he wasn't making any assumptions or taking any chances against the possibility of attacks. Snow was still falling at a moderate pace, limiting visibility and making him nervous.

He stayed close to Naomi as they headed toward his SUV. Once she was inside with the engine running and the heater turned on, he quickly cleared the windows of accumulated snow and then slipped into the driver's seat.

The feeling that things were about to ratchet up now that Jared was with the police—and could possibly give them information about some criminal activity he'd participated in or witnessed—settled over him. Of course, that was just Connor's working theory right now on why the siblings had been targeted. He believed Jared knew something that could get someone into serious trouble. What better way to force Jared to keep his mouth shut than to grab his sister and hold her hostage, threatening to kill her if he talked?

"I'll feel better when we get you settled back at the inn," Connor said as he pulled into traffic. "I mean settled in until we find the criminals," he added.

"About that," Naomi said as they approached an intersection and Connor made a turn. "I just want to be really clear that my staying at the inn, with you and the others, is because of the threat from the lowlifes who keep coming after me. It's nothing personal."

"Okay," Connor said, drawing out the word. Already, he felt the pang of loss in the center of his chest even though there hadn't yet been a new relationship between himself and Naomi that could be lost. Not really. Not beyond a version of friendship based on a past history together.

At least that's what he tried to tell himself. But the truth was, he'd thought there was something more between them. That maybe, in spite of everything, he'd fallen in love with her again.

Apparently, he'd fallen in love alone.

"Maybe you think I'm an idiot for even mentioning it," she said, rushing the words. "And I probably am. Protecting people and helping them out is part of your job. I know the fact that you're doing that for me doesn't mean I'm anything special."

Of course she was special. Way beyond special.

Even after the divorce and the years apart, it still felt like she was an emotional anchor for him. Maybe that wasn't the most romantic image, but it felt like part of the reason he was the man he'd become was due to the influence she'd had on him.

She'd given him a lot back when he'd been young and desperate for genuine caring and compassion in his life. He had no right to make selfish demands of her now. If she wanted him to let go of the hopes he had for a deeper relationship with her, he would let go. Or at least he wouldn't ask her for anything, wouldn't make her uncomfortable by putting his emotions on display.

Actually abandoning his true feelings for her might be too much to ask.

"Everybody loves a hero," he said, making a point to infuse humor in his tone even though his heart was breaking. "But when the movie is over, they want to leave the theater and get back to their real life."

"Exactly."

She wanted to be kept safe and after this case was closed she wanted to go back to living her normal life. Connor would do everything he could to make that happen.

And then he'd let her go.

THIRTEEN

"When I moved into my house I had no idea I'd be forced to move out barely nine weeks later." Naomi had spent much of the day following Jared's reappearance and arrest trying to maintain an upbeat mood for the sake of everyone around her. So far she hadn't been especially successful.

It was late in the afternoon and Connor was behind the wheel of the SUV driving to Naomi's house from the inn. Wade and Hayley followed behind them in Hayley's pickup loaded with plywood, tarps, a power drill and several other items to assist with the goal of getting the house winterized in case the hunt for the attackers dragged out through the season or even longer.

Snow had been falling steadily for the last two hours. "I'm sorry you're having to go through all of this," Connor said over the squeaking windshield wipers that were working hard to clear the glass. "But you know you're welcome to stay at the inn for as long as you need to."

The warmth of his voice and the kindness of his offer touched Naomi's heart. All the more reason to lock out the feelings they triggered. Exactly how she felt about him, whether those emotions were reliable, and to what extent she should allow herself to act on them, had all formed a solid knot around her heart that she simply couldn't untie. Not now. Especially not after the rude reminder of how foolish she'd been to believe that one man in her past had actually changed.

What an idiot she'd been to think she could trust her father. The pain over that realization hadn't faded. Might she be an even bigger idiot to think she and her ex-husband could actually have a future together? Be able to start something new and not be weighed down by the emotional baggage of their pasts?

She gave her head a slight shake, pushing away the questions crowding her mind and refusing to pursue them. *Enough.*

"I'm grateful for everything the Range River Bail Bonds team has done for me." She wanted to morph his comment into something less personal.

She'd been pretty blunt when they left the police station last night. She'd made a point of pushing him away. The words hadn't been easy to say, though she'd known it was the right thing to do.

Connor received an incoming call and he answered it on the SUV's hands-free device. "Maribel. Have you got some news for me?"

"Yes. I'm at the courthouse and the magistrate has declined to reset Jared's bail."

Naomi's shoulders slumped and her eyes rapidly filled with tears.

"She wants to talk to Detective Romanov about the situation with Kevin Ashton's murder. My guess is that she wants to be assured that Jared isn't a viable murder suspect before she allows him to get bailed out. The plan is for her to make her decision tomorrow."

"Got it. Thanks." Connor ended the call.

Naomi sniffed loudly and dabbed at her eyes. Then, with a flash of anger, she grabbed her phone and tapped the screen to call her dad's number. All she could think about was his stupid lie about seeing Jared and his pathetic move to get money from Naomi. No wonder old trust issues had flared to the surface. She set her phone to speaker so Connor could hear the conversation, but that turned out to be a pointless effort. The call went straight to voice mail.

"I'm sorry," Connor said quietly, acknowledging her disappointment and frustration.

This was something new and consistent, Naomi had noticed. Connor making the effort to speak to an emotional situation rather than ignore it. His comments might not be lengthy or particularly eloquent, but they were evidence of a genuine effort and they seemed heartfelt.

"Thanks." She looked out the window as he made the sharp right turn toward the Granite Bay community and ultimately her lakeside house. The house she'd imagined she would be living in and decorating whenever she wasn't at the factory supervising production and implementing plans to get everything at the facility updated. She was grateful that James had recovered from his injury and had returned to handling day-to-day operations until it was safe for her to go back to work. That was something she could do at this very moment: focus on things she was grateful for.

The SUV slid slightly in the turn despite Connor's careful driving. Having rainy weather so close to the temps dropping low enough for steady snowfall meant that there were lots of stretches of road with a layer of ice on them beneath the snow. Already, local news outlets were passing along the message from the county sheriff's department that people should limit their driving if possible tonight. The predicted big snowstorm had arrived and was expected to drop a couple of feet of snow over the next several days.

Connor cleared his throat. "So, Jack's informants weren't able to tell us anything about Almada or Olsen." He'd spent the majority of the day with Hayley and her husband interviewing several of his brother-in-law's informants. The bounty hunters had arrived back at the inn just in time to leave for Naomi's house before the roads got too bad. They hadn't had time to talk about the results of that outing until now. Naomi had pretty much figured that their efforts were a bust when they'd returned to the inn seeming subdued. Wade had agreed to come along and help with securing Naomi's house after Jack got a call from his own bail bonds company advising him that his assistance was needed immediately elsewhere.

"We're going to keep looking for them since they're bail jumpers and we're bounty hunters," Connor added, putting a little bounce in his tone in a clear attempt to cheer her up. "And you know the police department is working hard to find them, too."

Naomi was certain that as hard as the team worked, their efforts would bring out results sooner or later. She had grown quite attached to the Range River Bail Bonds team. She enjoyed getting to know Wade's wife, Charlotte, too. She was going to miss all of them—and the animals—when it came time for her to move out once the case was resolved. Her beautiful lakeside house would probably feel lonely after she'd gotten used to having someone around to keep her company anytime she wanted it.

Connor pulled into the driveway of her house and Naomi felt a jolt of panic that mercifully lasted only a few moments. But in those moments the fear and confusion she'd felt in the aftermath of the explosion four days ago seemed to be happening all over again. Connor unbuckled his seat belt and moved to open his door and slide out, and Naomi didn't do the same. When he noticed, he settled back into the SUV and closed the door. "You okay? You want me to take you back to the inn?"

"No." Naomi took a couple of deep breaths

and offered a silent prayer of thanks combined with a request for comfort and clarity. "It's pretty terrifying to think about the fact that the people who want me dead know where I live," she said softly. "And if they aren't captured, they'll eventually find me wherever I go."

"Wade and I will go inside and sweep the house before you go in. In the meantime, Hayley will stay out here with you."

"Thanks." They remained in the driveway and Connor restarted the SUV's engine so they could run the heater. They expected the others to arrive at any moment.

"I hate to say it, but we probably should focus our pursuit on your dad," Connor said. "Maybe we can find out what he's been up to criminally and check for connections with Almada and Olsen. I know Detective Romanov is already doing that, but as long as we don't interfere with her investigation we can ask around." He gave her a guarded look. "It's time we took a closer look at your life back in Las Vegas, as well. Maybe you have enemies that you aren't even aware of."

"It's all so bewildering." Not to mention exhausting to feel like danger was stalking her everywhere she went.

Hayley and Wade finally pulled up and

parked alongside them in the driveway. Connor exited the SUV to meet up with Wade while Hayley climbed in so she could guard Naomi. From Naomi's perspective, the idea of being protected was starting to seem hopeless. The attacks had come in a variety of situations. There was no way she could be kept safe at all times.

The truth was, if someone wanted to shoot Naomi right now through the glass of the SUV there wasn't anything she or Hayley or even Connor could do to stop them.

"I hope I'm not forced to stay in hiding for so long that I have to come back here to pick up my spring-weather T-shirts," Naomi joked as she came downstairs carrying two suitcases and set them by the front door.

Connor watched her as he gathered up various tools to put them back in a toolbox in the living room. The work Hugh and Maribel had done to cover the damage from the explosion the night it had happened was actually pretty solid and it had kept the interior of the house from getting weather damage. But considering the potential harshness of a North Idaho winter, he and Hayley and Wade had gone ahead and reinforced the existing plywood with yet another layer. After that, they had covered a few more windows near the explosion site with cracks that had gone unnoticed until now.

The truth was, it *could* take a long time until Almada and Olsen were caught and the case was wrapped up. Naomi might be staying at the inn for quite a while. And while a small, selfish part of Connor thought it might not be a bad thing having her close, the better part of him realized that would not be the best thing for her.

"As long as you're still alive when warm weather returns, I'll be happy." Connor froze as he was about to snap a latch on the toolbox. He hadn't meant to say that out loud. Slowly, he turned in Naomi's direction. She was staring at him and he felt his stomach drop. He'd said the wrong thing. He could almost hear the voice of his often-inebriated father telling him to watch what he said or else just keep his mouth shut. He opened his mouth to apologize but Naomi spoke first.

"Thank you."

That was not what he was expecting. For a moment he wondered if she was being sarcastic, even though sarcasm was typically not her style.

"You're right," she added, walking toward

him. "I want to be focusing on gratitude. The fact that I—*we*—have survived so much is an amazing blessing." She tucked her hair behind her ears and straightened her glasses.

"Amen," Connor said softly, his heart aching with love and admiration for the brave and strong woman standing in front of him.

He wanted so much to tell her how he felt about her, clearly and directly. But he couldn't bring himself to be that selfish. Naomi's life had been completely upended by the attacks and by her brother being framed for murder. Taking advantage of the moment and making this about himself and his feelings would be wrong.

Making a move at any point—even in the future—might turn out to be one of the biggest mistakes of his life. For the sake of not ruining everything, maybe he should just work toward maintaining a low-key friendship. Perhaps he needed to accept that the romantic relationship between them had ended years ago—for her, at least—and that it was never coming back.

Fighting the urge to reach out for her, to wrap his arms around her and hold her close, he instead bent down to grab the power drill and fiddled with the battery pack as if checking to see if it were secure before putting it in its case. While he was doing that, he took a deep, centering breath.

From the dining room area, where Wade and Hayley were busy cleaning up after making their repairs, Connor suddenly heard a voice speaking through a police radio. *"...repeat, the sheriff's department has released an alert to public media strongly recommending citizens stay off the road for the next twelve to twenty-four hours as heavy snow is accumulating on roads and highways atop an already existing layer of ice. Multiple slide-offs and accidents have all emergency agencies backed up, un-available to respond to calls. Be advised tow truck response is estimated at minimum three-hour delay."*

"Are you hearing this?" Hayley called out as she walked into view.

Connor nodded. "Loud and clear." He turned to Naomi. "You about ready to go?"

They'd already turned down the thermostats to levels low enough to prevent pipes from freezing without wasting energy. Naomi's car would be all right in the garage. The back patio furniture and barbecue had been brought in along with the outdoor hoses.

"We just need to check the boathouse," Naomi said. "I've got a couple chairs and a bistro table out there. I might have also left out a couple of throw blankets. Maybe something else, I don't remember."

"Okay," Connor said. He picked up his coat from the back of a chair and slipped it on. "I'll go grab whatever's out there and then let's go."

Naomi followed him to a back door. He pulled it open and snow showered down like a thick lace curtain in front of them. Heavy gray clouds hung low in the sky.

"I'll go with you," Naomi said, grabbing a jacket on a hook beside the door. "We can get everything in one trip. It would be ridiculous for you to have to go back and forth twice."

Connor glanced around the property from the back of the house to the barely visible water's edge. He didn't see anyone out there. The sooner he got Naomi back to the inn and off the dangerous, icy roads, the better. It would be quicker if she went with him and he didn't pull Hayley or Wade away from the work they were finishing up. He had his gun with him if he needed it—but there was no reason to think he'd need it. It wasn't that far.

Naomi had already started out the door so he shouted into the house for the benefit of Wade and Hayley, "We're going to secure the boathouse. Be right back, and then let's roll."

"Copy that," Wade called back.

Connor caught up with Naomi and then tried to get a little bit ahead of her so he could break a trail in the snow. While the depth of the snow wasn't a problem for him, he'd noticed that it was mid-shin level for Naomi and he wanted to make the walk—one that already felt more like a hike—easier for her.

While the weather might be uncomfortable, the view of the placid lake surrounded by snow-covered pine trees and nearby snow-capped mountain peaks was stunning. Connor had lived in Range River his entire life, yet he never took its beauty for granted.

"I think being born here spoiled me for living anywhere else," Naomi said as they neared the edge of the lake, breathing a little heavily from the exertion of slogging through the snow. "I had a good life in Las Vegas, but the whole time I couldn't help feeling like it wasn't really home. And like I wanted to go home."

A gunshot ripped through the peaceful quiet and Naomi screamed.

Connor spun in the direction the shot had come from, desperate to locate and neutralize the gunman hidden behind the curtain of snow.

Two men appeared suddenly, seemingly from out of nowhere. Both of them were wearing ski masks and both of them were charging forward in a full-out run. One of them lifted his hand and pointed a gun at Naomi.

Heart in his throat, Connor jumped in front of her to block the shot. Keeping his gaze fixed on the closest assailant, he reached for his own gun. "Run!" he called out to Naomi, but he didn't dare take his eyes off the shooter to see if she got away.

Seconds later, he heard her scream. It sounded like she was several yards away, but not in the direction of the house. Confused and scared for Naomi, Connor risked turning away from the gunman to look for her.

The second assailant had grabbed her.

Connor turned back to the nearby gunman. A split second before the assailant could fire again, the bounty hunter threw a roundhouse punch that knocked the man unconscious to the ground as the shot went wild, failing to hit anyone. Connor grabbed the dropped gun and spun around to run after Naomi.

The thug had her by the arm with a gun pointed at her head as he forced her toward the nearby expanse of woods that stretched to the lake. If Naomi was dragged into that tangle of forest and the storm grew fiercer, Connor might not ever find her.

He tried to sprint harder, but the snow slowed him down and patches of ice beneath it caused him to slide and threw him off-balance.

Drawing on every bit of strength and determination he had, Connor drove himself to move faster and get to Naomi. But he was too late. Right before his eyes, she disappeared behind the falling snow. The icy flakes dropping from the sky at a furious rate filled any footprints or trail that Naomi and the kidnapper left behind.

FOURTEEN

The gun had been pressed to Naomi's temple before she even realized one of the assailants had snuck up beside her. Now she was being dragged into the forest by a thug who had a painfully tight grip on her arm.

Her hopes had crashed as she'd been forced far enough away from Connor that he'd disappeared from view. Why the attacker hadn't just shot her, she didn't know. Maybe the goal was to get her away from the neighborhood and kill her in the forest where the sound of gunfire would be weakened by distance and the muffling effect of snow. Add that to the fact everyone would be inside their homes during this snowstorm, probably watching a TV or plugged into some other device, and no one other than Connor would have any idea something terrible had happened.

Was it Olsen or Almada who had hold of her? She didn't know. *Scream and you'll die right here*, the thug had said when he'd grabbed her. The mask had muffled his voice. It sounded familiar, but she couldn't quite place it.

Had the other criminal launched another attack on Connor? Her heart clenched at the thought of him being hurt, especially in the course of trying to protect her. It had taken this move back to Range River to truly understand that he had never stopped trying to protect or help her. All those years ago, when she'd felt he let her down, he'd actually been doing his best but hadn't known how to help her through her heartbreak.

Please let Connor be okay, she prayed, as a small flame of hope that she'd see him again flickered in her heart. She was certain that if he hadn't been injured and was physically able, he would try to find her, no matter what it took.

She would do the same for him.

She and the attacker were slowing down. The slog through the snow was difficult. Naomi was wearing ankle boots that weren't designed for hiking. The jacket wasn't meant for long-term exposure to this kind of harsh weather, either. The hood had long since fallen away from her head so her hair was soaked and she was sweating from exertion while also being chilled by the cold wind. She was exhausted and already shivering uncontrollably.

Soon, the exposure would leave her too weak to be able to make any kind of effort at all to save herself.

The kidnapper still had his gun, but he, too, was becoming fatigued and he'd let the barrel tip slip downward. It was clear he wasn't taking her toward a parking lot or a street or any place where he might have a vehicle parked to transport her elsewhere. This would be it for Naomi. Which meant she didn't have anything to lose.

Dear Lord, please protect me.

She couldn't fight the thug, but she could do something to make it easier for whoever might be looking for her to find her. With uneven ground beneath their feet and the snow falling so heavily, she and the attacker weren't leaving an especially easy-to-find trail.

She drew in a deep breath. *"Help!"* She yelled it as loud as she could. And then she yelled it again and again.

The thug yanked her arm and shoved the gun into her face.

She ignored the implied threat. At this point, what did it matter? She knew what he intended to do and she was not going to make killing her easy for him.

She flailed her free arm, knocking snow off of nearby trees and more importantly breaking the branches—leaving a clear marker that Connor could follow. She kept yelling as she flailed her arm, while at the same time kicking and stomping the snow and dragging her feet. Anything to leave behind even the smallest sign that she'd come this way.

Gritting her teeth, mustering all the strength she had left, Naomi twisted, hard, and managed to break free from the assailant's grip.

The lowlife cursed at her. Again, the voice seemed familiar but she wasn't going to waste time trying to figure out where she'd heard it before.

Her feet were numb with cold and her exhausted leg muscles were wobbly, nevertheless she ran as fast as she could in the snow. It was slippery going, but she quickly realized she'd surprised the kidnapper and gotten a head start on him. Determined to get away, she pressed herself to run harder.

Her boot slid in the snow—she tumbled sideways, fell and smacked her head on a big rock. The snow didn't do much to lessen the impact, leaving her dazed and disoriented.

The gunman grabbed the front of her jacket and yanked her to her feet, shoving the gun in her face again. *"Enough!"* he snarled. *"This is it!"*

Naomi swung at him, trying to knock the gun out of his hand, but she missed and fell again.

Through the mouth hole of the criminal's knitted mask she could see his teeth. She could tell he was smiling. Laughing at her, maybe. He shook his head, then aimed.

Connor appeared through the snow, moving so quickly that Naomi didn't recognize him at first. He came up behind the thug and the criminal turned around just in time for Connor to connect a direct punch to the loser's jaw.

The gun flew through the air and the man landed on his hands and knees. The criminal shook his head a couple of times before getting to his feet in a staggering stance. By that time Connor had taken the handcuffs from his utility belt. He grabbed the unsteady assailant's hands and secured the man's wrists behind his back.

"Connor!" Hayley yelled as she, too, appeared from the depths of the thick snowfall.

"Here!" he barked in return.

Naomi felt his reply more than heard it. Because by this time Connor had wrapped her in his arms and pulled her close to his chest. His heart was racing at a rate to match hers. In fact, it felt like their hearts were beating together.

"Are you all right?" Connor asked Naomi, finally holding her at arm's length to scan her for injuries.

By now Hayley had already taken control of the criminal.

"I'm okay." Naomi nodded, then felt a swirl of dizziness that had her leaning against Connor again. "Fell and bumped my head on a rock," she said by way of explanation.

"Well, you're okay, then. I know your head is harder than a rock."

Naomi laughed and it felt good. It felt like the laugh released so much—from years gone by to the horrors of today. She lifted her chin and smiled at him. He leaned down and placed a soft kiss on her lips. For a moment, she felt like she was getting dizzy again.

The press of his lips was warm and familiar and new and different all at the same time. He pulled her close again now, and continued to kiss her until she felt out of breath—which was fine with her.

When they broke contact she immediately missed his touch.

"I was so worried I'd lost you," he said. "For the second time, and forever."

"We've got to get moving," Hayley interrupted. "Wade's got the other guy. Cops should be at the house any minute. And you guys might not have noticed it—" a smile played across her lips "—but it's *cold* out here."

Connor took off his jacket and put it over Naomi's shoulders despite her protest. She turned down his offer to carry her back to her house, though.

Patrol officers were just arriving when Naomi, Connor and Hayley plus the attacker arrived through the back door. The attacker hadn't said much other than cursing and shaking his head. Naomi got the impression that he was still rattled by Connor's punch.

After being in the cold for so long, the warmth of the house felt like an embrace. Heavy exhaustion weighted Naomi down as she watched the bounty hunters hand custody of both attackers to the cops. Happy and relieved that everything was finally over, she watched with curiosity as one cop reached to pull the mask off the thug who'd dragged her into the woods. Was it dark-haired Almada, or the long-haired Olsen, both equally despicable for the murder of Kevin Ashton and the framing of Jared?

Her jaw dropped in surprise when the kidnapper turned out to be Tyler Copley, the man who'd competed against her to buy the furniture company. "I want my lawyer," he said.

The cop moved to the second thug, who dropped his face down and tried to look away, doing his best to avoid the unmasking, but it was no use.

"James?" Naomi said softly after his mask was removed. She didn't want to believe that the assailant was her employee, the manager who'd seemingly done so much to help her, a man she'd thought she could trust. "*Why?*"

"Don't talk," Tyler snapped beside him.

Instead of answering, James looked at the floor.

As the police completed the arrests and took everyone's statements, Naomi stood stock-still in surprise, dripping melting snow onto the tile floor. The shivering, which had stopped shortly after she came inside the house, started up again.

"Let me get a blanket to warm you up," Hayley said beside her. "Where do you keep them?"

Instead of answering her Naomi shook her head. "I don't understand why these people I trusted would do this to me." She turned to Connor. "And since these two obviously aren't Almada and Olsen, that means the attacks aren't over." It felt like the nightmare would never end. Connor wrapped his arms around her. His embrace already felt so comforting and normal. Almost like they'd never been apart.

"Let's not give up," he said, resting his chin on the top of her head.

For a moment Naomi wasn't sure if he was talking about the two of them, or about the crimes.

"Detective Romanov is very good at her job," he continued. "And that includes being good at questioning and interrogation."

Trying very hard to hold on to hope, Naomi hugged Connor tighter. And he hugged her back.

Nearly twenty-four hours later Connor walked out of his office at the inn and said to Naomi, "Detective Romanov just texted me. She'll be here in a few minutes."

"Has she found Almada and Olsen?" Naomi asked hopefully.

Connor shook his head. "I don't know."

Things between her and Connor had been tense since they'd left her house to return to the inn last night. At least it had felt that way to her. Once they were away from the immediate danger, once she was moving away from acting on emotion and instinct and was trying to be logical instead, she'd found herself emotionally distancing from Connor.

And he'd seemed to withdraw from her, as well.

Or maybe he was just respecting the boundaries she'd established after Jared was taken into custody? Back then, she'd been questioning her judgment because of her father. Now, thanks to Tyler and James, she had even less faith in herself. She'd even questioned if she really had the capacity to run the furniture business.

Afraid to go to the factory in person, she'd spent much of the day working online and had been happy to discover she had a production worker with excellent experience who was willing to oversee daily production at the Stuart Furniture facility for the time being.

The judge had set bail for Jared and after Connor took care of the bond Jared had gone back to his friend Robby's fishing cabin, where he felt Almada and Olsen wouldn't find him. Despite Connor's insistence that he would welcome him at the inn, Jared had declined to stay there. When Naomi spoke to him on the phone Jared had said he just wanted to stay in the cabin and lie low for a while. She had to respect his decision even though she wanted to see him. At least she could be fairly sure that he was safe at the cabin and wasn't falling back into bad habits.

Connor walked farther into the great room toward Naomi. She was seated on a sofa by the fire with a ragged and skinny tabby cat named Trooper snoozing in her lap. The critter was apparently a new arrival and when Naomi asked about it, Connor had claimed he had no idea who let the pitiful creature into the inn. Of course Naomi hadn't believed him. She knew what a tender heart the bounty hunter hid behind his tough exterior.

She knew she couldn't stand to lose him again. If they just stayed friends, and avoided the pull of a romantic relationship, then there was no chance they would ever break up again, right? Surely that was the smart choice. And yet, she craved so much more than just friendship—even as she was afraid of everything that could go wrong. When it all added up, it meant that right now she honestly didn't know what she wanted.

Connor sat down beside her. The cat opened his only eye and looked at Connor and then began purring. Connor reached over to pet the creature and looked like he was about to say something, but then his phone chimed and he glanced at the screen. "Romanov is here."

He went to let her in. Carrying the cat with her, Naomi headed for the office. Wade and Charlotte came down the stairs and also went into the office. And then Maribel joined them.

"We're all tired so I'll make this quick," the detective said after she was seated. She reached over to scratch Trooper on the head.

"Almada and Olsen are in custody." She looked directly at Naomi. "The threat to you is finally over."

Naomi took what felt like the deepest breath she'd taken since this whole thing began and blew it out forcefully. "Thank You, Lord."

Connor, who'd sat beside Naomi instead of at his normal spot behind his desk, reached over to take her hand and squeeze it. And he continued to hold on to it. "Where did you find them?" he asked the detective.

"Hiding out with a couple members of the Invaders. Not at their known clubhouse on

Tributary Road, but at a private residence on the back side of Wolf Lake."

"Why did they want to kill Jared and me?" Naomi asked, remnants of the fear and unease of the last few days still lingering in her mind like a dark shadow the sun hadn't quite chased away yet.

"Let me back up a little to give you some context," the detective said. "The Invaders got a foothold in our community fairly quickly and they made a lot of money in a short amount of time. They needed to launder their illegally gotten money and for a while they were able to do that through some small local businesses.

"Over time the Invaders' success made money laundering a bigger challenge. They needed a larger-scale way to launder greater sums. Someone in the Invaders had a connection with James Petrie at Stuart Furniture Company. Sadly, the former owner of the company had been in declining health for a while and he had entrusted the entire running of the company to James. James took advantage of that. In return for a sizable fee, he laundered money for the Invaders through the furniture company, and no one suspected a thing."

"James and the Invaders wanted me dead so

they could continue laundering money through the furniture company?"

"That's correct. As you know Tyler Copley is a self-employed accountant. He worked with the Invaders and helped them set up their money-laundering system. When Mr. Berger, the former owner of the furniture factory, announced he was putting his company on the market, Tyler thought he would buy it and together he and James would launder money for the Invaders."

"But Naomi bought the company, instead," Wade interjected.

"Right. And the Invaders' leadership—Hooper Cantrell, specifically—was determined to get control of the company because they needed it. Cantrell hired Almada and Olsen out of Las Vegas. He didn't want to use local professionals who might be recognized by the cops." Romanov looked to Naomi. "Apparently it's just a coincidence that they were hired out of the same town that you came here from. Anyway, Cantrell thought going after you directly would be a mistake. Your purchase of the company was a high-profile deal. If you were murdered, then whoever immediately bought the company afterward might be considered a suspect. He thought that if your brother was framed for a murder then you would get wrapped up in defending him and would be more open to selling the business because you wouldn't have the time to run it. Kevin Ashton was murdered for the simple reason that he was known to associate with Jared."

"But Almada and Olsen threatened me from the moment they saw me," Naomi argued.

"They were vaguely aware of the Invaders' ultimate goal of getting you out of the way. They got overzealous and thought killing you would please Cantrell. He wasn't thrilled when the hired hit men had just about succeeded in setting your brother up for murder when you arrived and the thugs turned the whole thing into a running gun battle—that they *lost*. At that point, Cantrell told Almada and Olsen that they'd blown the whole plan and now they needed to finish you off or he'd have his crew finish *them* off."

"So that's why they came so hard after me."

"The Invaders generally try to be clever. That's why it's been so hard for us to infiltrate them and bring them down. Until now. Now we have enough information to completely end their operation for good." The detective turned to Connor with the barest hint of a smile. Then the smile faded and she turned back to Naomi. "So, yeah, the new plan was to kill you to get you out of the way and then have someone in the employ of the Invaders buy the furniture company. It wasn't ideal since the new buyer would be under suspicion, but they figured they could find a way around that. Most of the attacks came from Almada and Olsen. Though the Invaders obviously used a few of their members when they tried to run you off the road. James locked you in the storage closet and set the fire. He only pretended that he was trying to help you. And his claim that he'd been knocked unconscious while trying to help you was a lie."

"So what was the reason for the attack by James and Tyler yesterday?" Connor asked.

"Cantrell thought the whole thing had gone on too long. He blamed those two for not closing the deal on the furniture company to begin with. He knew Naomi trusted James and told them they needed to kill you without any further delays or he'd kill *them*." Romanov turned to Naomi. "James knew where you were yesterday because you'd told him what your plans were. He let Tyler know and the two of them watched your house and waited for a chance to get to you."

"Wow," Naomi said, at a loss for further words. It was shocking to know this elaborate scheme had been going on all around her. And that she had been the target of a criminal motorcycle gang.

The detective got to her feet. "Between hard evidence, plea deals, civilian witnesses plus the acts witnessed and documented by our own undercover officers, we finally have enough to put an end to the Invaders and stop a whole lot of crime in this town."

"What about my brother?" Naomi asked.

"In return for his testimony on these recent events the bail jumping charges will be dropped. But he'll still need to testify in the drug-dealing case. And if he wants to keep out of trouble he needs to stay away from friends like that."

"He will," Naomi said, relieved and determined to get Jared back on the right path.

Soon after the detective left, Wade and Charlotte went upstairs, and Maribel retreated to the kitchen, leaving just Connor and Naomi in the office.

"Well, I guess there's no longer a reason for me to stay here at the inn," Naomi said. The threats had all been neutralized and thanks to the repair work done by the bounty hunters her house was certainly habitable.

The thing was, though, her lake home didn't hold the appeal for her that it once had. Maybe it was because of the attacks. Maybe it was because she'd come to love the moving waters of the nearby Range River more than the calm waters of Granite Bay.

"You sure you want to move back to that lonely house?" Connor asked with a slight grin and tilt of his head. He seemed sure he knew what she was thinking and it would be annoying to tell him he was right.

"My emotions are all over the place right now," Naomi replied, deciding to speak plainly because that was what she wanted from him. "You've started to grow on me a little bit. And I know you feel the same way."

He smiled broadly and reached for her other hand, too.

"But I think we might need a little time to figure this out," she continued nervously. "Time when people aren't trying to kill me and the situation isn't so emotionally intense."

"Why can't we work through all of that while you still stay here?"

She shrugged. She couldn't come up with a good answer—probably because she didn't really want to. She liked living at the inn with Maribel and Wade and Charlotte and all the animals. And Connor.

"Whatever you want to do, we'll do," Connor said. "If you want to move back to your house and date for a while, I suppose we can do that. As far as I'm concerned, we can date all the way up to our wedding day if you want."

"You're pretty sure of yourself." Naomi laughed and Connor gently pulled her hands toward his back until her arms enveloped him. Then he leaned down for a kiss and she melted into him like a patch of snow in front of a fireplace.

He released her hands and wrapped his arms around her waist, pulling her closer, all the while maintaining the kiss.

Finally, he took his lips away from hers. She already wanted him to put them right back.

"I love you," he said. "I'm pretty sure I always have."

Naomi's eyes filled with tears.

"We're good together," he continued. "Even after all that's happened in our pasts and our time apart, we still have a connection you can't deny. We both have faith now. We have life experience. I finally learned how to talk about feelings, which wasn't easy." A self-conscious smile played across his lips. Then his expression became more serious. "We'll make a good husband and wife."

"I can't argue with that," Naomi said. So she didn't. She leaned in for another kiss, instead.

EPILOGUE

Six months later

"So how does it feel being married to Connor again?" Maribel asked with a wide smile.

"Wonderful!" Naomi answered, grinning. "It feels both new and familiar at the same time," she added a little more thoughtfully. *Exciting and reassuring, as well.*

Naomi had just walked into the kitchen of the Riverside Inn. She and Connor had gotten married in a small ceremony the day before at the Still Waters Church in downtown Range River. The reception had been at an Italian restaurant on Indigo Street. It was a low-key celebration with the feel of a family gathering even though plenty of people had been invited who were not literally members of their family. It had been just what Naomi and Connor wanted.

Naomi's dad had not responded to her invitation, but Jared had been there along with his close friend Anjelica from the coffee shop. He'd stayed on the straight path after having the charges against him dropped and had come to work for Naomi at the furniture factory.

"Good morning." Charlotte greeted Naomi as she squeezed oranges for fresh orange juice.

The plan for this morning was for a big celebratory breakfast with the family. Jared should arrive at any minute. Danny and his wife, Tanya, were already there as were Hayley and her husband, Jack. And of course Wade and Charlotte already lived at the inn.

One of the dogs sat at Connor's feet, staring at him adoringly, while Connor made a fresh pot of coffee.

Good thing the inn was large and had so much room. Even better that Naomi was married to a man with a big heart who lived to help others—people and critters—without stopping to count the cost.

Naomi walked up behind Connor and wrapped her arms around him. He took one of her hands and kissed it while continuing to fiddle with the coffee. She grinned, fully aware that he was intent on brewing the freshly ground beans because he knew she loved them.

They would leave for a honeymoon in the Bahamas next week. Neither of them had been in a particular hurry to get away. Both of them craved the feeling of being with family. Especially with Connor worrying that his siblings, now that they were all married, would move on with their lives and he'd see less of them at the inn.

Naomi didn't think that seemed likely. The siblings and their spouses appeared to like hanging around here a lot, which was fun.

She headed toward the kitchen counter, heavily laden with Belgian waffles and strawberries, scrambled eggs with cheese and onions, homemade biscuits, sausage and bacon, and all sorts of delicious-looking things. She was searching for something she could do to help when Maribel took her by the arm, then took Connor by the arm, and pulled the two of them out of the kitchen, through the great room, and out to the deck, where she'd already set up a table with a tablecloth and lilacs in a vase. "You two lovebirds sit here. The rest of us will bring out the food."

Connor pulled out Naomi's chair and then sat across from her, his eyebrows raised. "Maribel's stronger than she looks. I guess you know that now."

Naomi giggled in response; her heart filled with giddy joy.

Very quickly the food was on the table in front of them and the family was seated around them. Maribel offered a prayer of gratitude.

When it ended, Naomi and Connor looked up and locked eyes for several seconds. By now, they were comfortable with that feeling between the two of them that went beyond words. The one like Naomi was feeling right now, when the connection between them felt like something that had always existed and had never been broken.

She shifted her glance to the nearby Range River flowing by and the bright sparkles of sunlight dancing on its surface.

So much time had flowed by with the two of them living completely separate lives. Yet it had taken that time apart to bring them back together.

Naomi set her hands on the table, sliding them toward Connor. He reached for them and gave them a gentle squeeze. A moment later he leaned across the table to kiss her—and of course she leaned in his direction and met him halfway.

For a lot of years she'd lived in a desert and missed Range River; the river itself as well as the lakes and streams and lush green forest. For the last couple of years she had found herself wanting to come back. In this moment she realized that what she'd really wanted was to come *home*. And she was home now.

* * * * *

If you enjoyed this
Range River Bounty Hunters book
by Jenna Night, pick up the previous
books in the series:

Abduction in the Dark
Fugitive Ambush
Mistaken Twin Target

Available now from
Love Inspired Suspense!

Dear Reader,

I love to see families brought together in stories—through marriage and also through beloved friends who become family.

I also enjoy seeing people learn and grow—especially when boosted by the power of faith—and reaching a point where they can forgive, receive forgiveness and then move on. That's what happened with Naomi and Connor.

Thank you for joining me in the pursuit of bad guys in the Range River Bounty Hunters series.

Please sign up for my newsletter at jennanight.com to get the latest updates on my new releases. You can also receive book release information by following me on BookBub or Facebook. And if you're so inclined, feel free to drop me a line at Jenna@JennaNight.com.

See you next time!
Jenna Night

HARLEQUIN
PLUS

Try the best multimedia subscription service for romance readers like you!

Read, Watch and Play.

Experience the easiest way to get the romance content you crave.

Start your **FREE TRIAL** at
<u>www.harlequinplus.com/freetrial</u>.